Chapter 1

A Cruising Rally

"There is no ideal age, but I know that if at all possible the best time is now, as tomorrow may be too late"

"I gotta feeling, uuuuuh, that tonight's gonna be a good night, that tonight's gonna be a good night, that tonight's gonna be a good, good night." The music was thumping, the crowds were singing along to the CAR anthem at the top of their voices. It was the Cruisers' Atlantic Rally's opening ceremony at the Baha night club in Las Palmas, Gran Canary, and the mood was close to ecstatic.

"Have you heard about the weather?" Susie from Bavaria 38 "Möwe" yelled at Carla and Hanna over the loud music, pulling her new friends into a quieter corner of the night club. "No, is there a new forecast?" Norwegian skipper Hanna sounded unconcerned. "I just called our weather man in Kiel; the forecast for the start Sunday is a shocker. 45 knots on the nose. I'm not sure we will go out in that," Susie said. The petit, blonde German in her early sixties looked anxious. She and her husband Hans intended to sail across the Atlantic as a husband-wife team, hard work in any conditions. And their Bavaria 38 was pretty elderly. "Hurricane Sandy is messing up the weather patterns we should see this time of the year. But at least we are here. Think of all those boats still stuck in Gibraltar, they might not even make it to the start." Hanna tried to calm her friend's nerves. Susie had only started sailing five years ago, this rally was her husband Hans' dream, and right now she was not sure she shared it.

"I'm really worried about the kids and me being sick the whole way across, wouldn't that be awful?" Carla knew that they all got sea sick on a regular basis. Her children had been fine on the trip down from Gibraltar, but they had mainly motor-sailed in flat waters. "A strong headwind would certainly knock us around, everybody would be spewing for sure. How will I cook and look after the kids and the rest of the crew while feeling sick?" she sighed, turning towards Hanna. "Not that you have those worries."

Hanna Anker smiled sympathetically. A professional skipper who chartered out bunks to adventure-hungry sailors on her German-Frers designed Swan 51 "Thea", she had done the crossing nine times before, the first time as a 10-year old. But she also had a duty to her customers, and eight sea-sick punters would probably not recommend their voyage to friends. Norway was a small country, and news spread fast in the sailing community.

"If the weather is going to be that bad, I might also delay my departure for a few days," Hanna mused. "But clearly that would ruin "Thea's" overall result, and I do want to win my bet against Pavel on his Hanse 52 "Gdynia" this year. Also my old Swan would revel in the heavy windward conditions." Carla admired her new friend's courage and attitude. She was so professional, and to handle that big, heavy boat and have the responsibility for all those people was no mean feat. Carla had never crossed an ocean before, and tried not to think too much about how it would be like for real. There was no turning back now.

The CAR community was only starting to get to know each other. Some boats had arrived in Las Palmas weeks ago, others had made it just in time to join the festivities during the two weeks before the start. The boats were spread out on several docks of the vast marina, and the sailors mainly connected to boats around their own berth and at nightly gatherings.

In a quiet corner of the bar several incorrigible smokers clustered together. CAR veteran Rudi patiently explained to one of his crew, a small dark-haired Italian woman: "With any two boats meeting on the water, a leisurely cruise turns into a race. The CAR - although a rally - has a racing division and also a rating system for the cruising participants, and let me tell you, some skippers can get quite competitive. But we will just cruise and have a good time." He had started out crossing this ocean on a tiny wooden boat, but now aged 71 he could afford an Oyster 56, a luxurious cruiser. And was never short of people who wanted to go sailing with him. Over the shoulder of his companion, Rudi noticed an Asian man with yellow died hair sucking his cigarette, eyes nervously darting around. The man's crew-shirt said "Saiche," maybe a Chinese competitor, they were everywhere now, he thought.

Cruising rallies were a booming business. The magazines were full of new rallies launched, the latest by rally veteran Dale Foster from Lanzarote to Martinique in direct competition to the CAR. In contrast to decades earlier, when people opted out of their land-based life for good, sold all and went cruising, the short sailing sabbatical was en vogue. One year break from normality, maybe even three. Some people with very little experience just bought themselves a 50-footer and set off. Rally participants believed sailing in numbers was safer than alone, but the truth was, the ocean was vast, and in the end you had to be confident to solve your problems alone. A lot of sailors took part in the rally for the camaraderie, parties and life-long friendships formed.

This year's 27th CAR with around 260 entries was bigger than ever, the largest trans-ocean sailing event in the world. First organised by cruising legend Dale Foster, it now lay in the capable hands of Rally Cruising Pty Ltd and its blue-striped team. Over 200 boats started every year at the end of November in Las Palmas, Gran Canary and sailed around 2800 miles in 15 to 23 days to the Caribbean marina Rodney Bay in St Lucia.

Chapter 2

Carla

A few CAR participants woke up a bit fragile the next day, but the morning was glorious, finally sunny after days of rain and cold. "Do you need crew?" a disheveled man in his mid-thirties accosted Carla outside the gate to dock, that could only be opened with an access card. The ageing hippie with matted hair introduced himself as Poldi from Austria. He started speaking German to Carla as soon as he heard her accent, but his put-on Austrian charm didn't distract from his unkempt looks. Poldi said he was looking for a berth across the pond, some obscure story about retrieving his boat in Hawaii. Carla politely shook her head: "Sorry, we are full." But Poldi was not the only one looking for a ride. Legions of young amateur and professional sailors were walking the docks to try and find a boat sailing to the Caribbean for the work season there.

"Darling, I'm just going to the marina office to see whether the spare filters have arrived from Mallorca," Carla yelled down into the companionway where Steve was crouched in front of the open engine compartment. The kids were playing Lego and drawing at the saloon table and could not get out, as Steve had removed the companionway ladder to get to the engine. "That engine is his real baby," Carla thought resigned. "But as we need it for power, navigation, lights, communication it better work all the way across." She turned left off dock L and was almost skipping, enjoying the feeling of going off on her own.

Carla and Steve May from Sydney were on a one-year sabbatical and had been on the boat for seven months now. They had signed up for the CAR knowing there would be like-minded families with children, so their kids Leif and Frankie, now ten and seven, would have a fun time before and after the rally. And more confidence on the ocean, knowing their friends were out there too. On Carla's insistence they had had an expensive SSB radio installed by German expert Jörg from yachtfunk.com, so the children could take part in a kids' radio net on the ocean.

It was a long walk for the 36-year old mother of two, but she didn't really mind, having been stuck below decks all morning sorting out their floating home. Swan 46 "Dania" was full of things collected on their journey around the Med, as well as school material, toys and games and whatever else was needed to keep two children happy and entertained. Carla knew she had to pack away lose items before heading into the Atlantic swell. At least the final homework had been sent off to the Distance Education School in Sydney that morning, the kids were on holiday now.

This was the last, most challenging part of their sabbatical. Carla truly hoped it would turn out to be the experience of a life time for all of them. In this rare moment of solitude she thought about the past months, and had to admit, it hadn't all been smooth sailing, especially things between Steve and her. Living in such a confined space with your husband, kids and at times her elderly parents without an escape had been surprisingly difficult, and there had been plenty of rows between her and Steve. About trivia, mainly mooring the boat, how high to hang the fenders, not getting a line across quick enough, how much engine maintenance was needed. The list went on. Carla had to admit the boat was very difficult to steer and Steve did a great job, but sometimes the tension and responsibility got to him. The kids had started to say: "Stop fighting, you two," which was no good at all. They had never fought before in their marriage, life on the boat seemed to bring out the worst. The crossing would be a real test. But so far Las Palmas had been great and the preparations unrushed and smooth.

Muello Deportivo, as the marina was called, featured a tunnel on the south side toward the old town and a ramp into the shopping district on the north side. The shops and restaurants along the marina road

Joaquin Torrent Blanco were built beneath the six lane elevated highway, Las Palmas' traffic artery. To get to the marina office Carla had to walk around the whole marina.

"Hi, Basil," Carla waved to a Sydney sailor, who was having a coffee opposite dock L. "Do you need something from the office, I am going over now?" Look for some mail for me, will you, thanks." the Australian replied. The Sailors Bar was very popular, Cuban waiter Carlos served proper sandwiches and delicious pasta, and the CAR office in makeshift containers was conveniently located opposite. The office had only opened the day before, and sailors stood three-deep at the counter waiting to register or ask questions.

"Have to tell Steve that the CAR office is open now, he should get our name down for an early safety check," Carla thought out loud. Her very precise Steve had insisted on getting their safety gear organised while having some maintenance work done months ago in Turkey, although it had meant spending a disruptive week in a boat yard. When the boat is your home, having tradesmen trample through your limited space is often reason for marital strife, as many women cruisers can confirm. But Carla had to admit that the long week in Turkey would hopefully pay off now. Steve had confidently declared that he was ready for the safety inspectors. Life raft and life vests, EPIRB and retrieving devices all had an up-to-date stamp. It had cost a fortune, but was all necessary, naturally.

"Lorraine, how good to see you, you are covering the rally again? Looking forward to the gear test, always really informative!" Lorraine from yachting magazine "Regatta" stood outside the container chatting to CAR boss Liam. Carla knew her from a boat test they both had attended years ago, when Carla was still working as a journalist in Europe, centuries ago, before she had met Steve and had the children.

“Let’s go guys, shoes on, grab a jacket, we don’t want to miss any of the fun!” Steve was herding his family off the boat. Tonight was the first CAR kids gathering at Club Veradero for all families. While the children started a table soccer contest girls against boys, the parents put their feelers out. Who would they become friends with, who was a good match for their kids. Conversations flowed, stories were compared. ”So you are from Stockholm, how much time have you got off, are you going all the way?” “How are you going to school the kids?” “You were in that gale on the way down from Portugal, you poor things, how did the children cope?” Steve stood in a group of men comparing boat preparation stories while Carla kept an eye on Leif to see how he went with the other kids. Just before their departure the nine-year old had been diagnosed with Aspergers Syndrome, a light form of autism, and the family was still coming to terms with it. Right now Leif happily took part in a chip eating competition with an English boy, and Carla turned toward a group of mothers.

She just heard Sabine from Germany say: ”I quit my really good job as an investment banker to be able to go on this trip. If I had let him go by himself our marriage would not have survived I think. We won’t be in the CAR, though.” The other women looked confused. Sabine explained with regret in her voice: “My husband does not believe in group things, we will just follow you a day after the start.” She looked a bit sheepish, as her husband was clearly enjoying the “group thing” tonight, talking to the other skippers. Sabine also feared that they would be a bit lonely without the CAR roll calls and communication. Carla got the feeling the parents had not been alone with their children for such a long period of time. “I told him our youngest at two years was too young for such a trip, but he wouldn’t listen,“ Sabine sighed. “Take plenty of entertainment for the kids, you can’t have too many toys,” Carla smiled sympathetically. Spontaneously, she decided to confide in the other woman: ”You know, I sometimes long to be back home soon and get some space from my family. Living the dream can be hard work."

The party only finished at ten pm and adults and children happily strolled toward their jetties. The guys and kids were crowding around a vintage VW Kombi when Carla saw hippie Poldi walk past the bar with a backpack, was he sleeping rough?

Chapter 3

Old Rivals

Pavel was not having a good morning, to say the least. The Polish skipper of "Gdynia" sat on the dock in front of his boat, steaming. A short email at 8 am had ruined his chances of making a profit on this trip. A group of four customers had cancelled their booking this morning, very late and in breach of their charter contract, but what was he going to do, sue them now? He had stretched his budget to the limit buying his Hanse 52 earlier this year, and had no money for lengthy law suits. Pavel was sure the guests had counted on that. "Gdynia" slept ten, him and his first mate Andre included, and now he was four guests short. That meant almost 5000 Euros less. He knew his father, the senior partner in his business, would be angry.

And amongst the remaining four guests one already seemed big trouble with his endless demands and foibles, still in his bunk with a hangover at this hour. Pavel was not really looking forward to this crossing, especially with the weather forecast getting worse by the minute. "Andre, what about the rigger, is he coming or not?" the skipper yelled at his first mate. There should be no problem with a brand new boat, but on the rough crossing from Gibraltar the lower spreader had broken off, just like that. Andre had spotted it straight away and they managed a crash tack, but it had been a miracle that the rig hadn't come down. Now Pavel was haggling with the boat yard about warranty payments.

Not that he was short of a quid in general, quite the opposite. Born into a working-class Polish family Pavel Wessolowski's luck had turned when his electrician father, a member of the now famous Solidarnosc movement, had been awarded the Nobel Peace Prize with his friend Lech Walesa and two other shipyard workers. When the German wall came down and the Soviet Union collapsed, his father had seized the opportunities the new Poland offered and had quickly become wealthy. From a two-bedroom apartment in a prefab block to a villa in the best suburb of Gdynia had not even taken five years. And Pavel as the only child reaped the benefits. School had been a drag, Pavel preferred extra-curricular activities like driving around in his sports car, chasing girls and sailing. The girl side of things had come easy to him, with his tall frame, floppy blonde hair and charming smile he could get any girl, at least that's what he thought. But when his father had bought a holiday house on the Baltic and then a yacht, Pavel soon became hooked on sailing. Last year after lengthy, not very easy discussions, his father had agreed to help him set up a charter company with the new Hanse. He controlled the money flow, wanted Pavel to work hard and make a success of it. He knew the working hard bit was always a bit of a problem for Pavel.

The only female skipper in this rally, and Pavel's main competitor, was having a better day. Hanna Anker from Oslo in Norway had had "Thea's" rig checked, collected the No 5 genoa from the sailmaker and had booked the safety inspection for the next morning. Now she was taking a break, curiously looking at the Chinese boat alongside her Swan 51 "Thea". The all-carbon Asia 60 "Saiche" looked fast and very modern. Open stern, chimed hull, mast far back, small headsail and coffee grinders, a bit much for the CAR. But maybe this was a test to see how the boat and its material would perform under the strains of an ocean crossing, Hanna mused. Nobody seemed on board. "They might be in a hotel, the lucky people," Hanna thought. Not blessed with the typical Scandinavian look of blonde hair and an amazon figure, Hanna nevertheless possessed striking looks. Slim but muscular with a wild mane of brown curls controlled by a headscarf she was never short of male suitors, but aged 28 hadn't settled down with anybody yet. She had a reputation of solid competence and was widely accepted by her male colleagues in the charter world. By all bar one, unfortunately, the stroppy Pavel. Last year he had skippered a wealthy Russian's Oyster 57 across and had beaten Hanna by half a day. Not this time, she promised herself.

Hanna had teamed up with her childhood friend Elsbeth for this crossing, or maybe childhood friend didn't describe their relationship that well. Elsbeth had been Norway's top Optimist sailor before Hanna joined the youth racing scene aged 12 and blitzed it in her first season. She had pushed Elsbeth off the podium as the youngest Norwegian Optimist champion ever. The two girls hadn't spoken for years afterwards. However, when Hanna advertised for crew for her first charter trip on "Thea", right after her father's fatal accident, to her surprise Elsbeth replied to the ad and said she wanted to come on this sail across to Scotland. The girls had worked well together, and Elsbeth had been on a few more charter cruises when she could take time off her business degree.

It had taken Hanna years of therapy to come to terms with her father's death. Her mum had died giving birth to her, and her father had brought her up, in his unconcerned, unconventional way. They had led a gypsy life in her younger years, lived on their boat, her father had raced a lot and worked on other people's boats. When Joern Anker had been offered a delivery trip to Antigua on a 20-meter ketch he had not hesitated to take his ten year old daughter on her first Atlantic crossing. Eventually, her father had become manager of the most prestigious Oslo yacht club and they had moved into a caretaker cottage.

Hanna had been on an advanced Yachtmaster course in Fiskebäkskil when the phone call came. Her dad was missing from his Swan 51 "Thea" on a booze shopping trip to Skagen, Denmark with some friends. He had been alone on deck late into the first night and must have gone forward to adjust something at the mast. He somehow had fallen overboard and was not wearing a life jacket. By the time his watch relief appeared in the cockpit he was gone. Joern Anker was never found. The thought of her dad in the cold water, knowing for sure that he was going to die, almost drove Hanna mad. Years of working through this accident with her psychologist had made her accept the nature of his death to some degree.

Hanna's charter guests would arrive this afternoon. She had been extremely lucky this time. Her six guests would not be from all walks of life, a motley bunch finding out about their bad habits and character traits on the high seas, but the sailing committee of a North German sailing club, all experienced sailors and very good friends. "This could be one of the easier rides," Hanna said to Elsbeth.

Chapter 4

Happy Hour

"Frankie, sweetie, do you want to help me with the laundry?" Carla was dragging the big laundry bag up the companionway stairs "Mummy, no, Sophia is coming over and dad has promised we can go up in the bosums chair." "Have fun, darling, I'll be back in an hour or so." Carla was lucky, bumping into her friend Kirsten climbing off the boat with two big plastic bags of laundry herself. Shared pain was half pain. "God, do you remember the fantastic laundries in Spain, Greece and Turkey," Carla reminisced while she loaded her bag onto a trolley, a rare find on the dock. "How a huge marina like Las Palmas has no marina laundry service is beyond me. In other places sailors can drop their salty and sweaty clothes to some friendly industrious people and get them back fresh, clean and folded." "What I hate most are the coins, a ridiculous system," Kirsten added. In Las Palmas sailors had to get a truckload of coins from the chandlery and then spend hours processing clothes through washing machines and dryers. They could not even use their own laundry detergent, Carla's daughter Frankie already had a rush on her bottom from the chemicals.

When Carla and Kirsten entered the laundry they breathed a sigh of relief, three machines were empty, a good start. Quickly they loaded them and started feeding in the many coins. "Why don't you go back to the boat, I will text you when yours is through." Carla offered, and Kirsten happily went off. Carla settled in front of her machines with the recent Ken Follett. Not a bad way to spend an afternoon.

Forty minutes into the washing cycle the door opened and two Asian women entered, looking shy and unhappy, carrying three big duffel bags of laundry. "Let me help you with that," Carla offered, but the older of the two women just shook her head and looked down again. "Another half hour and you can get some machines, just come back," Carla said friendly. The younger one of the two nodded and without a word they left.

"Marcel, have you got time to drive me to the post office?" Carla hours later asked the owner of a formerly bright red Ecume de Mer on dock L, now faded pink. The boat looked as if it hadn't left the marina for decades. Frenchman Marcel helped yachties with errands, information, and even offered two old Peugeots for car hire. He was part of the marina furniture.

"What's the story with the Chinese," Carla couldn't help asking when the Peugeot was stuck in Las Palmas traffic. Although a mere housewife now, her journalistic instincts were still intact. An economist and finance journalist by profession, she had done lots of yachting articles in her little free time in the last few years. Poorly paid bread-and-butter stuff, though, no real scoop that could help her get into the workforce again after their trip.

"A bit odd, not sure what is going on, the women seem to be more or less slaves and never smile, I have seen some young sailors as crew, all Chinese, and an older sailing master with an attitude. I have heard the owner will arrive in a few days. He is the boss of the boat yard." Marcel knew.

The first happy hour drinks on the grounds of a little sailing club right next to the CAR container was already hopping when Carla and Steve arrived with their kids at 6.30. The eerie green light from the canopies shone on sailors standing in little groups, enjoying their two free drinks. The kids played near a little bridge at the water's edge.

"Cheers, Carla," Australian sailor Basil clunked his glass at hers. He had been there right at the start, when Carla had met Steve. The happy group of sailors chatting around the big bar reminded Carla of the Clipper Bar in Porto Cervo, where she and Steve got together during the Swan Cup. Basil had his Swan 44 moored next to Carla's boat "Bella Gioia" then, he had become a firm friend. So much had happened since then, her move to Sydney, the kids, buying "Dania" and finally the long planned sabbatical, culminating in the CAR and Christmas in the Caribbean. How lucky was she!

She had started sailing when she was ten. Her long-suffering mother had given her sailing-mad father an ultimatum then: "Either you buy a family boat or I will get a divorce." They had sailed as a family ever since, and when Carla came into a bit of money she bought her dream boat, a S&S Swan 40 from 1972. She had raced "Bella Gioia" in Porto Cervo in her chaotic first year of boat ownership and had met tall, lanky engineer Steve there. He had started racing when at university and had co-owned a Swan before, sailing on a friend's Swan 48 in Porto Cervo. They were very well suited and sailing was their life. Carla hoped that all would get back to normal between them on their return to Sydney. "Cheers, my darling," she smiled at Steve and clinked glasses. He smiled back and kissed her on the cheek.

Steve had tried to convince their jetty neighbors Henk and Kirsten from Dutch entry "Andante" to tag along to the Happy Hour, but they were still recovering from a shocking crossing from mainland Spain, where a new engine had been installed into their brand new Botting 48. The hapless Spanish mechanic had managed to flood the new engine with salt water during the trials, and although it had been flushed and they were assured all was good, when Henk had tried to start it in the busy entrance to Las Palmas harbor it had not fired. An English boat noticed their distress and had towed them in. Now Henk was making a list, prioritizing the repair work and worrying, how so close to the start it all could be done, while his new friends were socializing in the makeshift bar in a boat storage area.

"Want another drink, girls?" one of the Taylor brothers, Peter, offered to go to the bar for Hanna and Susie who were chatting animatedly. Born in the sailing mecca Cowes on the Isle of Wight, the three brothers Peter, Chris and Nick were all handsome, but charter skipper Hanna thought Peter, the eldest, particularly attractive. And she never ran out of conversation with him, Peter had started sailing as a child, as she had. With a smile he handed her a fresh glass of champagne and started to say something, when somebody exclaimed: "Look at that idiot on the stage, he thinks he looks so cool!" A tall man swigging from a Jack Daniels bottle with a cigar in the corner of his mouth had joined the band on the small stage, trying to dance with gyrating hip movements.

"That is that German guy Thomas, he won't take part in the CAR, out of principle he says. He has that amazing new X55. Will start a day after our start, don't know how he got in here without a CAR door pass, he looks pissed," Peter said. "Ah, that do-gooder," Susie's husband Hans from "Möwe" knew. "I have read about him in a German yacht magazine. Former corporate lawyer. He will take his two small sons, a teacher and his wife across the pond, and in the Caribbean help the natives, something with water." "Kellermann, komm da runter," another German yelled at the drunken sailor to get him off the stage. The friends lost interest and turned away to resume their conversation.

Polish charter skipper Pavel was already on his fourth beer and queuing for the next when Hanna pushed through to the bar. "How are things, Pavel," she smiled, "good crew this year, everything ready?" "You bitch," Pavel slurred. "You know dam well that my rig is still not fixed and I am short of crew, so just shut your stupid mouth!" Taken aback by the intensity of his dislike Hanna did manage to say: "Well, looks like this year I might beat you then." Peter Taylor, now next to her, protectively pulled her back towards his brothers. "Is that how you speak to women in your country, you loser, I suggest you apologize to Hanna quick smart." Pavel took an uncoordinated swing at Peter, but missed and stumbled forward. Peter with one sharp blow to Pavel's solar plexus felled the Pole and turned toward the others, rubbing his hand with a smile. "Boxing at Bryanston does come in handy sometimes."

Peter and his brothers had all attended the reputable English boarding school Bryanston in Dorset, with their parents based on the Isle of Wight. Sailing had been integral part of their home and school life. The family spent their summer holidays in Salcombe, Devon, with their grandparents. Gramps Taylor was running the local sailing school from the club's barge at that time, and soon all three boys had their sailing instructor ticket. Nick had joined the family firm while Chris became an accountant, but Peter had the sea in his blood and became a Super Yacht project manager, based in his home town Cowes. The brothers' Atlantic crossing on the Pogo "Crazy" had been a bar joke last Christmas when they had all hung out at the Island Sailing Club, but they were all game and it was great to sail together again.

Still staring at the bar where a minute ago the conflict had escalated, Carla suddenly heard children screaming. "Mum, mum, Samuel has fallen off the roof and is really bleeding!" her daughter Frankie rushed up to her. "Right over there, at the slipway!" Samuel, aged seven, was one of the wilder boys from the UK and Carla ran off to find his mother. "That will need some stitches," mother Lisa expertly wiped the blood off Samuel's chin, "can somebody organize a car to go to the hospital?"

Chapter 5

Rally Preparations

Marina showers are a dying breed. Most modern yachts are now lavishly equipped with separate showers and a water maker to feed them. Sailors that live on more classic yachts, however, could describe the best and worst shower experiences they have had in marinas in detail. Bad, disgusting or cold showers were the bane of their cruising life.

The Las Palmas marina showers had simple wooden benches along the walls, half open tiled cubicles with two water knobs. The one working shower out of the three shot first cold, and then very hot water at its victim. At least the half open cubicle had a hook for the towel and a shelf for shampoo. "In the ranking of marina showers of the world it gets 4 out of 10," Carla mused, trying to get the shampoo out of her long, straight blonde hair. "I should have it cut shorter before we head out, would be more practical," she thought to herself, critically examining her sunburned, freckled face in the mirror after towelling off. Turning around she almost bumped into Sabine, the former banker from Germany. What was she doing here, surely they had a luxurious shower on their 55-footer. It was hard to be sure but did Sabine's eyes look really red, maybe from crying? "How are things, how are the kids?" Carla asked.

Sabine looked on the floor and sighed: "I just had to get away for a bit. I am struggling to keep the kids busy while endlessly shopping for the crossing, helping with getting the boat ready and so much else, it all seems too much. Our teacher has quit today, I couldn't believe it, so now we have to sail two up. And Thomas is so demanding." Her face looked worried and tired. Carla tried to cheer her up, chatting about the upcoming parties, but it didn't really work. "Are you going to the provisioning seminar, we have to hurry, it starts in ten minutes."

The CAR seminars were all well-run and interesting, most sailors attended them. The provisioning session, expertly presented by CAR expert Chloe, led to a general panic, though. "If your rig comes down your crossing could last up to four weeks, you need to provision for that." she lectured. More food, we need more food, the fleet's cooks or skippers headed to town again, shopping at El Corte Ingles. Thank god the department store delivered onto the jetty right to the boat.

Much more pressing problems were on Sven Martens' mind. The boyish German boat builder needed to rustle up some money to pay for the provisions for his hungry crew of twelve. He knew, his brand new Hanseatic 60, the pinnacle of the family's boat building career, simply had to make positive headlines in this CAR, and ideally sell straight after the crossing. Otherwise bankruptcy was looming for the 150-year old family business on the German river Elbe. The boat was also called "Elbe", slightly old-fashioned for such a modern and innovative boat, Sven had thought, but his mother had insisted. "Our boats have always been called "Elbe", your father would have wanted this one to carry the name too." The name was the least of Sven's worries now, he wondered who could he call for a short-term loan, maybe his Aunt Elke.

"Hey, Sven, Alter, wie geht es Dir?" Sven Martens, outside the seminar venue Real Club Las Palmas, turned around toward a friendly German voice. His old school friend Soren was beaming at him, Jesus beard, ponytail and all. Sven couldn't believe it. "What has it been, five years, what are you doing here?" Sven embraced his old friend. "I am helping some Chinese get their boat across, as their tactician," Soren looked slightly sheepish. "Oh, no, my direct competition, what a shame, I hope they pay you well." Sven was disappointed. Soren was a born sailor, had grown up on the river and could get any boat to sail fast. If the Chinese boat reached St Lucia first all the media coverage would be about it. And the Martens yard so desperately needed good PR for their flagship. Sven had only just managed to pay out his two brothers and their sister after their father's sudden death, but as a consequence the yard had a serious cash-flow problem. More so as the development of the 60-footer, his baby, had been delayed and very costly.

Hanna had just finished putting on the main sail after its check at the sailmaker with Elsbeth, her co-skipper, bone-breaking hard work, when British hunk Peter from Pogo "Crazy" stepped on board with a six-pack of beer. "Ready for a happy hour drink, ladies?" he bowed and gave them his dazzling smile. "You are a life saver, we have run out,"Elsbeth replied, grabbing a bottle of Corona. The three of them settled in the cockpit with some cheese and biscuits. "Hey, Asimov, get away from that chicken pate!" Elsbeth shooed the boat's cat away. Cats and dogs were not that unusual on boats, although a pain, Elsbeth thought. At least cats did their business on cat litter, dogs and toilets could be a real problem on long crossings. There was a massive Golden Retriever on a catamaran on this year's CAR, Elsbeth was glad they only had the male ginger cat. Hanna's father had given her Asimov for her 18th birthday and Hanna was terribly attached to the animal. The charter guests didn't seem to mind and Hanna had put an allergy warning on her website.

"What is the name of the yard that has built that rocket next door," Hanna asked Peter, glancing over to the Chinese entry. "It is not Far East, right?" "No, the yard is China Star in Quindao, and they are really expanding, trying to copy Far East's success. They also started with Optimist dinghies like Far East but soon decided to aim higher. They are new to building in carbon fibre, it will be interesting to see whether the boat, an Asia 60, will hold together in the forecast conditions. This carbon racer is supposed to catapult them into the league of McConaghy or Green Marine, they are under enormous pressure to perform. Their financial backer is some Chinese billionaire, maybe the yard owner Michael Lin will even skipper the boat with its all Chinese crew himself, but they have a German tactician." Hanna was as always impressed about how much Peter knew about the industry, but in his role as Super Yacht project manager he was well connected and received a lot of information about the yachting industry worldwide.

China was by now in the top ten of boat producing countries with more and more boat yards establishing themselves, Peter explained to the girls. Initially a sport for a few Chinese millionaires yachting was now hip in China. China's Guo Chuan's solo non-stop circumnavigation had made headlines in 2013. Guo then led a Chinese crew successfully through the North East passage, Peter said. "Here, I've just read the article in this old Yachting World," Elsbeth grabbed the magazine and read out loud. "After 13 days of racing on the treacherous waters of the North East Passage for 3240nm, Qingdao China, led by Chinese skipper Guo Chuan, finally crossed the finish line on the Bering Strait at 16.48 UTC September 15, 2015. Skipper Guo Chuan and his five crew from Germany, France, and Russia completed the journey. For the very first time in history, a racing trimaran sailed non-stop successfully through the Arctic Ocean Northeast Passage from Murmansk to Bering Straits." "Amazing stuff, they are on a roll. The history of boating in Western countries shows that when per capita income is about $3300 the industry develops. When the figure reaches $6,000, it starts to boom. China's per capita income is now $4000," Peter concluded.

"Thanks for the lesson on China and sailing, but how about another beer and let's talk about the weather for the crossing, Mr-know-it-all!" Elsbeth demanded. "Look at that! What a poky little thing, you would have thought they have proper dive gear, he has been down there forever," Hanna, distracted, stared at the little yellow dive-generator on the next deck with its pulsing black hose. Obviously somebody was working below the water. "Now that is a beautiful boat, I wouldn't mind having a closer look at the Hanseatic." "I will organize it some time, I know the owner," Peter smiled. "Come on, girls, let's drink up and get Chris and Nick from "Crazy" to go to town for some tapas and wine."

Two hours later strolling back from a great Spanish meal Hanna and Peter were walking behind the others toward the pedestrian bridge over the still busy road, discussing the pros and cons of a parasailor spinnaker. Peter's brothers had taken good-time girl Elsbeth onto a tour of the town's night clubs but Peter and Hanna had quietly agreed on a night cap on "Thea". Behind them a man suddenly started shouting, they turned around to see what was up. A tall figure was gesticulating toward a woman dragging along a small boy on each hand. "That is Thomas, the German with the X55,"Hanna whispered, "maybe I can hear what he is saying, I had German at school for years." She took Peter's arm and slowly they strolled on. "He is talking about money as far as I can understand, and something about building works, no idea what it's about, wasn't he a main player in the tree planting ceremony this morning somewhere on the island?"

Chapter 6

Mask Ball

"Do you want to come along to Carrefour, Carla?" Carla looked at the mess around her and didn't hesitate to escape it. She was trying to stow away the just delivered mountain of food into the already jam-packed cupboards of "Dania", when her Dutch friend Kirsten shouted from the dock. A true cruising boat, their Swan had lots of storage, but it was never enough. In sole charge of provisioning in her family, Carla was still missing a few special food items and had not been to the French supermarket yet. The women climbed into Kirsten's hire VW Golf and drove toward the south end of the island. "I have seen it on the other side when we came back from our island tour." Carla said. "Oh, there it was!" They had spotted the store too late and had passed the exit. "Let's take the next one, no problem," Carla tried to soothe her slightly nervous Dutch friend.

Kirsten was supporting her husband Henk every step of the way in his boat preparations, but their Rolls-Royce of a Dutch boats, a Botting, had severe technical problems after a new engine had been installed in Spain. Kirsten was driving around all day every day to source spare parts, and now was on a quest to buy some drinking water, as she was worried about their aluminium tanks contaminating their water on the crossing. Henk and Kirsten were expecting their son to arrive the next day to join them.

The Carrefour was a bit out of the way, the frantic CAR shopping centred around the market hall and El Corte Ingles. But the French supermarket turned out to be worthwhile with its shelves full of delicious food, some of it imported from France. Carla soon was filling up her trolley. "Where to put it will be the challenge," she inwardly sighed. In the International section she noticed the three

Chinese women from the laundry bending over a meat fridge. "How is your shopping going, how many do you have to feed on the crossing?" Carla tried to strike up a friendly conversation. The women turned toward her startled, even looking anxious, but Carla smiled encouragingly. The youngest one in the end answered: "We are eight people, need lots of food. Do you know where we can get good meat, this is not what we want?" Carla was in the middle of explaining the location of the best butcher in the market hall when the young woman tensed up and stared over Carla's shoulder at somebody approaching. A middle-aged man with yellow hair was giving a short, sharp order in Chinese. "Sailing master, have to go," she whispered toward Carla as they moved away quickly.

The afternoon on "Dania" zoomed by. Steve was fiddling on deck with their recently arrived crew Josh and Nathan while Carla packed away the food. Frankie and Leif had art classes in the boat's saloon with American artist Cindy who had offered to teach them how to draw. Later a Danish girl came to visit and the kids took turns in swinging off the rig in a bosum's chair on a halyard.

Steve had finally gotten hold of the handicap list issued by the organisers. "Dania"'s rating looked promising, he saw relieved, the ratings officer had clearly taken her shorter rig and centreboard configuration into account. Those special features made her slower than other Swan 46s. The racing division had some serious players entered who wanted to win the event, but that didn't mean that the skippers in the cruising division were less ambitious.

The CAR mask ball that night was staged in a night club at the far end of the marina, and the CAR organisers were pleased to see that people had really made an effort with their costumes, some were barely recognizable. Venetian masks, koala outfits, and a whole doctors team, what a hoot! The music soon got louder, kids and adults were sweating on the dance floor.

"Steve, my man! Can we wrap you in toilet paper, put you on a stretcher and pretend you are an accident victim?" Swiss sailor Marco in his green doctors' outfit beamed at Steve. 'OK, then," Steve gave in, "Carla, can you please take some photos of this." Frankie and Leif were laughing their head off when they saw their mummified father on a stretcher being carried through the night club. Around 11 o' clock Steve and Carla left the party to walk their children back to the boat. They bumped into Hanna at the exit. "Hey, you two, we'll have a nightcap on "Thea" with a few people in half an hour, why don't you join us?" "Great idea, see you soon," smiled Steve. Swan people stuck together, they had met Hanna soon after their arrival in Las P.

A few hours and glasses of wine later Carla was heading back to the boat alone to check that the kids were all right, leaving Steve on "Thea". Carefully climbing off the Swan's stern onto the big boat dock she heard a heated argument out of the open companionway of the Chinese yacht to port. Against her better judgement she wanted to hear what was being said, so stood very still in a dark spot on the dock close to the boat and tried to eavesdrop.

"This isn't working, you can't do this, it is dangerous, I won't allow it, "an accented voice was making a point. "You are being paid to do a job, so just do it," another man answered. Somebody stormed out of the companionway, jumped off the boat and landed on Carla. She tried to grab something, anything, the boat's rail, the person's shirt. With a big splash she fell backwards in the water, missing the harbour wall by an inch. God, it was cold! When Carla resurfaced she could make out a big hand and was being pulled up. The tall man with his ponytail looked at her angry but distracted, he had a somewhat wild look about him. "Who are you, what are you doing here?" he asked. "I was just stepping off 'Thea' here," Carla answered with a sheepish look. "Sorry, I did not see you there," the guy said, turned and hurried away. A bit rude, Carla thought, although it clearly had been her fault. What had been said hadn't made much sense to Carla either, but might mean the Chinese boat was planning something that was not in the rules. "We better stay out of their way," Carla thought while walking to dock L, shivering and dripping. "But one shouldn't be prejudiced against them just because people believe Asians are overly competitive," she mused. There was a lot of Non-Asians that were trying to bend the rules in any sport, just look at cycling. All men were racers at heart, Carla believed. Even her steady, calm Steve had grabbed the first handicap list with the ratings when it came out and then stormed off to the regatta office.

The next morning Carla was surprised to find an expensive-looking padded envelope in the cockpit, almost like a wedding invitation. On opening it she found a posh invite to a boat launch. Carla had put her name on the media list although not active as a journalist here in Las Palmas. "Darling, look at this," she handed Steve the invite with a big grin on her face. "Veuve Cliquot all afternoon. They are sponsoring the Chinese boat and we are invited to the official launch at 4pm, Carla May and guest, that is you, haven't been to one of these in ages. What fun!" As Carla well knew "Saiche" was moored next to "Thea" so they had no trouble finding the boat. About fifty people had already gathered on the quay under the bright orange sponsor flags. On the bow of the boat stood a few Chinese in suits and the uncomfortable looking guy with the pony tail that Carla had collided with.

Carla and Steve grabbed a glass of French bubbly and listened to yard owner Michael Lin telling them about the boat. Carla noticed Sabine and Thomas Kellermann in the crowd. Lin finished his speech with the words: "Unfortunately urgent business commitments won't allow me to take part in the race, but I have complete trust in our skipper Li Yang and tactician Mr Soren Meyer here, as well as our crew who will lead our outstanding boat to victory." "So much for the rally spirit," Steve whispered to Carla, taking another glass of champagne.

Chapter 7

Countdown

The atmosphere at the Saturday briefing was tense, to say the least, noise levels high, skippers and navigators nervously exchanging information. Carla, sitting between Steve and Hanna, felt she was not the only one spooked by the approaching weather. Some of her friends almost hadn't made it to Las Palmas due to the heavy winds and high seas. Hurricane Sandy in the US wreaked havoc unexpectedly late in the hurricane season, and the trade winds did not seem established. After some introductory remarks by CAR boss Liam Winter, weather man Chris quickly gave an overview over the development in the next few days, no good news there. More than 40 knots on the nose expected for the first two days of the rally. People looked seriously worried. CAR boss Liam took the microphone again, and announced:" Only for the second time in the CAR history we have decided to postpone the start, the cruising division will not leave until Tuesday. The racing division will start as planned tomorrow." His short speech was met with stunned silence. Then the crowd roared with relief, the applause was deafening. What a great decision! The organisers knew how to keep their customers happy.

Carla turned to Steve with a huge smile on her face and said: "I can't tell you how glad I am. Finding your feet in the ocean bashing into a gale would have been a horrible start to the trip. The kids and I will be seasick for a few days whatever the weather, but the delay will hopefully mean the swell will have calmed down a bit. I will cook two stews for the first days and hope for the best." Sailing since the age of five, Carla could do very little against her seasickness. She also got car sick, even got dizzy moving her head too fast. It had never stopped her from sailing, and big doses of vitamin C plus some Stugeron often helped. But looking after two sea sick children and cooking for three men would be a serious challenge while feeling nauseous.

At midday the next day a procession of cruising sailors walked up the Las Palmas promenade toward the Old Town to watch the racing division start. Carla and Steven had teamed up with some older New Zealand sailors, former Admirals Cup participants, who knew the best spot from where to see the start close by. Steve organised a few beers and they settled on some benches. "Why is that Chinese machine not in the racing start, and also that beautiful new Hanseatic? Are they trying to win our cruising division, that is not fair?" Carla asked no one in particular. No sign of the heavy winds yet, the start was slow and the racers drifted southward. After a fun tapas lunch in the Old Town with the Kiwi sailors Steve and Carla spent the afternoon hanging around the boat not doing much at all. Before the special happy hour the CAR had put on, the "Dania" family walked the humming docks where brass bands were playing and wished their many new friends a safe journey. They were ready!

Sven Martens that afternoon sat in the cockpit and leafed through his list book. "All good, skipper?" his friend and right hand Mogens Meier, nicknamed Mogli, joked. "As good as it can be without a proper budget," Sven sighed. "Can you check the new preventer system for me, Mogli, and we'll get the crew together for a briefing this afternoon. I will go ashore for a moment and get something."

Pavel had finally had some luck. The rigger had, oh wonder, turned up at the last minute, knew what he was doing, and a test sail had shown that the rig was well tuned. The start delay meant he had more time to finish boat preparations. He was going to beat that uppity Hanna on her old tub, he was sure of it.

On the little Bavaria “Möwe” Hans and Susie took a break together in the cockpit, sipping a cup of Ear Grey. “It is a bit late to say but I am not sure I can do this,” Susie said in a small voice. “We’ll be all right, my girl, just don’t worry so much,” her husband tried to soothe her fear. “But if you want to I will try and get somebody to join us, there has been many young sailors walking the docks, maybe I can find somebody suitable.”

The start! At 10am Tuesday “Thea” left the dock like everybody else. It was complete chaos. Hanna waved at Susie in “Möwe’s” s cockpit, the Germans had decided to leave late and start at the back of the fleet to stay out of trouble. One hour to go til the start! A ten-boat wide and 50-boat long queue was trying to squeeze out of the marina. It was tight! The Dutch boat “Andante” was right behind Hanna, getting a bit too close. Henk and Kirsten had gotten the boat somewhat ready, hopefully the technology would hold together. Hanna expertly got her boat through the marina entrance without a collision. Her crew hoisted the main in the traffic exclusion zone, something was flapping, they had to lower the sail again, pulled it up for a second time and now got into trouble with a police boat for drifting into the restricted zone. Finally Hanna bore away and headed for the line. A rain squall went through, visibility was poor in about 20 knots of breeze. Everybody was in full wet weather gear with life vests on. “This weather was not in the brochure,” one of the German crew joked, “this is just like home!”

The Chinese racer “Saiche” was zooming up and down the start line as if starting to the Volvo Ocean Race. “What is Soren thinking, these guys are dangerous,” Sven Martens behind his big carbon wheel turned to his tactician Ole while tacking away. The Chinese boat was reaching through the cruising fleet at top speed under full main and No 1 head sail. “Let’s keep out of their way, we hang around the pin end, this is a rally, not a race, we have a long way to go," Ole recommended. Also, if starting too early, extra time was added to the result, unnecessary pain.

A bit further back in the second row the Cowes brothers' Pogo "Crazy" tried to get away from under the wind shadow of "Gdynia", both boats charging toward the line with over seven knots. "Too close, Pete, too close" Nick Taylor from the bow signalled to port, "He is bearing down on you, watch him." "Up, up, up," Peter shouted at Pavel. The Pole should have steered to windward, the racing rules were clear here, but Pavel was just staring straight ahead. The two hulls now had just a foot between them, and one little wave from the side would make them touch. "What is he doing? Pete, bear away!" Chris cried out, but it was too late. Pavel had turned the wheel to port and a sickening crunch went through "Crazy" when the huge Hanse scraped along the Pogo's side. Peter spun the wheel away from "Gdynia" while his brothers were already checking out the damage. "What an idiot, that was totally avoidable, the new paint job ruined, we have to protest him," Chris was hanging over the starboard side inspecting the hull. Pavel had sailed on without a glance at the other boat.

"Stick to that guy Pavel on the Hanse, he knows what he is doing, just follow him" the annoying Swiss guy Urs tried to guide Hanna. "What a tosser, how dare he," she thought but bit her tongue and instead wove her own path through the crowd of boats. Urs was a late notice addition to her North German crew, as one of the Germans had fallen ill and had to cancel last minute, very unfortunate, as know-it-all Urs was already winding Hanna up. Two minutes to go, "Thea" was near the front, Swan 51 "Northern Child" pushing past from behind with their huge genoa, very powerful. And there were her friends on "Dania", right there with the professionals, well done Steve! Hanna unfurled the No 3 jib and headed for the line. "Bang," the start, they were off. "That worked really well," Hanna thought pleased. Next to them sailed an Australian Amel, a

Norwegian Swan 44 was right behind them, they were looking good. "Thea's" bow pointed to the southern tip of Gran Canary toward the dunes of Maspalomas, closely following the match racing leaders "Hanseatic" and "Saiche", until they couldn't see Las Palmas any longer.

Chapter 8

Early Days on the Ocean

Dania

"First, the ocean, the steep Atlantic stream. The map will tell you what that looks like: three-cornered, three thousand miles across and a thousand fathoms deep, bounded by the European coastline and half of Africa, and the vast American continent on the other side: open at the top, like a champagne glass, and at the bottom, like a municipal rubbish-dumper. What the map will not tell you is the strength and fury of that ocean, its moods, its violence, its gentle balm, its treachery: what men can do with it, and what it can do with men." Steve was reading to his children at bedtime, normally just whatever kids book they wanted, but tonight, the first night on the Atlantic he wanted to share Nicholas Montsarrat's quote from "The Cruel Sea" with them. It was eight o'clock and the day had been exciting for everyone. Day one of a big ocean crossing is always challenging, and this was only the second time the kids had been on a longer trip offshore. Steve did not want to frighten them but still make them aware of the enormity of was they were experiencing right now.

On any crossing skipper and crew have to establish routines and watch systems, get used to the rolling of the boat, overcome sea sickness and begin communication procedures. On "Dania" they were now six, their little family plus Nathan and Josh, two guys in their thirties who would share the watches and make manoeuvring the 20-ton boat easier. Carla started a daily diary. For the first entry she wrote: "After our good start we sailed close to the coast and at the higher-wind acceleration zone on the Southern end of the island put a reef into the main sail. A pod of grey-pink small dolphins played around our bow, cute. Everybody ate some red soup and tried to settle into the motion. During the first night nobody got any real sleep because the boat was pitching and surfing so much in up to 40 knots of wind. The waves were huge, quite scary, and we still saw lots of CAR boats sailing into that first night."

Thea

"OK, guys, let's do another safety briefing. Everybody knows the rules?" As a veteran of Atlantic crossings Hanna had firm systems in place that Elsbeth and herself had hammered into the crew before departure. That was: into all but Urs, who had only arrived on the morning of the start and had not seemed very interested when Hanna gave him a private safety talk. She had been firm: "The main rules are, everybody in the cockpit is clipped on, you only move to the front clipped on and with somebody else present, nobody pees over the side, that's what we have toilets for, no alcohol before happy hour at 6, you consult me before any manoeuver, always turn the big black switch off before turning on the engine, and on it went..." Actually, nobody had even felt like having a drink that first Happy Hour, they were too busy getting used to the boat's notion. "I think it is complete over-kill to have to wear life vest and harnesses in the cockpit, do you really think we will fall out?"Urs looked at Hanna defiantly.

A very early Frers design, the Swan 51 had beautiful lines with a low freeboard, but sailed like a submarine, waves washing over the deck into the back cockpit unhindered. The Germans in their heavy duty wet weather gear didn't mind, they were used to uncomfortable conditions so everybody was still in the cockpit or on the middle deck after dinner. Elsbeth on the helm grinned at Hanna who was climbing into the cockpit after a position and weather check. “Urs got soaked to his underwear, right through his lightweight dinghy jacket and jeans, what is he thinking.” The Swiss sailor quickly disappeared down below not to be seen again that night. Hanna always stayed up the first night, resting at the chart table when necessary, to make sure the people in her care were coping and safe. A watch plan was stuck next to the companionway with a list how everybody liked their tea and coffee. A hot beverage was being served to the new watch in their bunk when the previous person woke them up.

Gdynia

The high winds and swells that first night made a few boats go back with gear failure, very disappointing after long months of preparation. For Pavel’s German Hanse this was the first real test sail in the ocean. “Gdynia” had been trucked from the German yard to Villefranche only six weeks ago; the trip from the Cote d’Azur to Gibraltar had seen the usual light winds of the Med, and they also had to motor-sail for long periods from Gibraltar to the Canaries ahead of that low that many of the other boars got caught out in. “She is not very stable on the rudder, swerves quite a bit,” Andy dared to tell his boss Pavel at the end of his first watch. ”Rubbish, she is all right” Pavel hissed, “and now put one of the punters on the wheel and help me with dinner, that’s what they pay for, first hand ocean experience.”

Dania

Day two was still windy, but the breeze had backed off to about 30 knots and the fleet had spread out. Most boats could still see one or two other boats on the horizon. Having been fairly miserable all morning, Carla later on recovered from her seasickness. After the morning radio sched she managed to chat with Kirsten on "Andante". "I tried the SSB for weather information, can't manage it yet. The kids are in bed, Leif is quite sick. The rest of us had soup for lunch. How about you?" Talking about mundane things made Carla feel a bit better, distract from the noise of the heavy boat pushing through the waves at great speed. "Dania" was trucking! In the afternoon Nate caught a little tuna that made five filets. Another tuna bit the lure, but got thrown back as he was too small. The fish went straight in the freezer, Carla didn't have the stomach to fry up fish that night. Toward the evening "Dania" had slowed down a bit, and they changed onto a westerly course following their weather router Wetterdienst's instructions. Carla was snuggled into her lee cloth in the starboard bunk and wrote: "No dinner for me, guys eat ginger beef, kids are weak. Frankie spoke to her friends Sophia (Sirius) and Emily (Rafiki) at 7pm on the SSB kids net, she was thrilled, it works really well." The night went by without problems. The moon and stars were out for the night watches, Carla saw two, three boats on the horizon, and everybody got some sleep.

"I have managed to send emails to race control and home after hours of trying with the SSB," Carla proudly told Steve during next day's morning watch, time they spent together in the cockpit. "Well done, darling! Amazing technology, old but good," Steve smiled at her pale face. "We'll be fine then, that's a relief. No surprise that the Tailasail email via satphone doesn't work, I didn't think the service guy was very switched on."

The 1pm radio sched where boats had to report their position as well as weather and events turned into a shambles as two net controllers tried to get the positions at the same time. After the sched Steve got on the radio and called Peter Taylor and an Australian skipper to hear some gossip. "Tallulah Ruby has broken her boom fitting," Peter could tell him, "and there was a row between our radio controller and the Chinese boat's tactician, he didn't want to report their position, said they were safe and sound and that's all he needed to know. That's against the rally rules."

Möwe

"Are you sure about this Northerly route, Poldi," Susie Müller asked the Austrian hitchhiker with a nervous smile, peaking at the massive following swell out from under "Möwe's " dodger. "Only, I've heard that further North you can encounter headwinds, and we were quite keen on a downwind run, more like a milk run as they call it." On the old Bavaria life had changed quite a bit since they had taken the globetrotting Poldi as third man on board "to make life so much easier for you on the crossing" as Poldi had promised them one evening in front of the dock gate. Initially Hans had been grateful for Poldi's help in getting the boat ready, but now the Austrian had sort of taken the boat over and was acting as if he was the skipper. Hence the decision to take the most Northern route, even above the rhum line. It could get hairy up there, Susie knew, and their old girl and the two of them, now in their sixties, were possibly not up to the challenges ahead.

Hans agreed: "Head south until the butter melts and then turn west if you want an easy passage and get into the trade winds blowing from behind, this old saying has been true for hundreds of years." Some years, however, the trades were not fully established this early in the season. Lone passage makers often went after Christmas when the weather was more stable. But rally organisers wanted their customers to arrive in the Caribbean just in time for Christmas, with relatives and friends flying in for the festive season and to greet the sailors. Poldi wouldn't budge. "We will be much faster if we take the Northern route. I thought you wanted to be there by Christmas and celebrate with your grandchildren, it won't be a problem, I'll do everything." Hans and Susie exchanged an uncertain glance, how had this happened, after all the preparation they seemed to be mere passengers on their own boat.

Chapter 9

Routines in Place

Apart from the weather briefings rally control was supplying before and during the rally, participants had different ways of getting additional weather information. Steve from the wild coasts of Australia was determined to get excellent weather information and hence had signed up with a German weather service. Following a detailed forecast before the start their weather router would email them a forecast and route recommendations with waypoints every few days. They had told him beforehand what sort of crossing they wanted, fast but with winds from behind, no more than 25-30 knots. So a middle course would be the likely scenario for them.

The Australian family was doing really well, Carla was so relieved. The evening routine on "Dania" for the whole crossing had been established once nobody was sick any longer: The whole crew had dinner around 6pm, Carla then put the kids to bed and put her head down herself while the boys washed up and somebody stood watch. During the night they also ran single watches, the autopilot was on all the time, nobody hand steered. Steve took the watch before Carla from 10pm to 12 pm but hardly ever had to wake her, she could somehow feel when it was time to get up. Carla was on from 12 to 2, then Nathan. The person heading off watch wrote some wind, miles etc. data into the ship's log before lying down.

Carla did not like night sailing in general, she found it hard to see in the dark, and it was difficult not to fall asleep. The boys listened to music in the cockpit at night, but Carla did not want to get distracted from the boat's sounds. "Dania" was surfing down the Atlantic swells at more than 10 knots and the person on watch had to constantly tweak the autopilot not to risk an involuntary gybe.

Naturally Steve hat set a preventer, even to the bow, but an accidental gybe always put strain on the gear, you had to be careful. Carla blinked her eyes, ahead it was pitch dark. “Another half hour,” she thought, “I am so looking forward to my warm bunk.” She got up, looked ahead, turned around to the sides and tried to pierce the darkness, watched the back for a while where water was noisily gurgling in their wake, there, what was that? Another boat, right behind them, with no lights, Carla could make out the dark hull and the sails. Were these people crazy to come so close? A big wave could lift them and they would hit “Dania”. Carla hesitated for a moment, should she call Steve up. What could they do, call the boat on VHF? Then, to Carla’s immense relief, the boat gybed its headsail and main and turned onto the other gybe away from them. She had not been able to see a sail number or boat name, but could see it was a big monohull with a modern shape. Hopefully that was all the excitement for this night.

Carla continued to write in her diary: “Day 3: Thursday, Nov 29 at 4388nm. In the morning shook reef No 3 out to 1 ½ and ran full No 3 jib. We got much better speed. 8am breakfast, Frankie in the cockpit, all feeling better. Beginners mistake: during the night two bowls of stew on the carpet, one thermos flask broken, three bowls of muesli in the sink, one mug handle broken off, lots of bruises. The rolling has been not so bad from night two onwards, but the odd wave throws the boat around just when you are moving hot beverages or try to dress or undress. Down below is a haven of calm, all you hear is the sound of water slushing or racing along the hull. I have not had the stomach yet to start turning the vegetables in the nets above our bunks like instructed. The first few days the kids slept and drank a lot but eat very little, especially Leif. The soup and stew lasted for days, which was great for me. The boys are really good with kitchen duty. On day three some of the capsicum is getting wrinkly so I am thinking about chicken fajitas. In the afternoon during Steve’s watch the rod started to reel and soon Steve handed the rod to our "youngster" Nathan to reel in a medium sized Mahi Mahi with a yellow belly. A lot of Aquavit was needed to sedate the struggling fish that made fantastic dinner. The kids were super excited and afterwards unfazed watched part 3 of "Lord of the Rings". We are going well!"

The days came and went and the fleet had settled into the rhythm of the ocean. The wind still blew heavy on the Northern route, stabilized around 25 knots on the rhum line and went light further south. An ocean crossing has a special routine, down to life's basics, watch keeping, food and sleep in the framework of the watch system, some four hours on, four hours off, some only two on and six off, some boats with one crew in the cockpit, some with two. And for bigger manoeuvers all hands on deck, out of the warm sleeping bag, into oilskins and life vests and onto the deck.

On "Dania" the children had overcome their sea sickness, played games and drew pictures, looking forward to the afternoon when all off-watch crew watched a movie like "Pirates of the Caribbean". Carla had been worried that time on the crossing would pass very slowly, that after a week everybody would be completely over the whole thing and just want to get ashore. But that was not the case at all. The days flew by, were not boring and rarely stressful and all were enjoying this special time on the boat. She had been unlucky, on her own in the cockpit one morning a fish had taken the bait and by the time she had reached the rod the whole gear had been pulled overboard. No more fresh fish on "Dania". Carla was also glad that the boat that came so close that first night had overtaken them and was now just a few miles ahead, they could see it most nights.

"Steve, listen to this," Steve woke up from a confused dream when his wife shook him just after 2am. "After my watch I have listened to channel 68 on low volume, a boat called "Traction" has hit a container, is holed near the bow and is sinking, a major rescue operation is underway. But they are too far behind us, I have looked at our position, I don't think we can help." Steve quickly compared the pencil crosses on the chart and agreed with Carla. The stricken boat was about 50 miles behind them, no way could they beat back to it in time to be useful. "A Spanish freighter is trying to pick them up, they hopefully will be fine, but it sounded as if they had to get into their life raft soon." Anxiously Carla stared at her husband looking for emotional support. Her worst nightmare during dark nights in the ocean was hitting a sleeping whale or a container at great speeds. Shipping lines lost thousands of containers overboard each year. It was nothing a yacht could take precautions against. Every crew had an emergency grab bag near the companionway, one could just hope never to need it. "This is not the sort of trade wind rally I had imagined," Carla sighed and looked at Steve. "Several incidents already, even if we are ok it is stressful to hear, I hope all this will calm down now."

Chapter 10

Wrong Choice

Möwe

Susie slowly came out of a deep, happy dream. Somebody was shouting, why? She was still glowing from the inside, warm and snug in the port saloon bunk, still seeing the pictures of her two granddaughters in front of her inner eye, the little girls she had dreamt about just a minute ago. But reality was seeping through her hazy head, there was so much noise. The noise of the wind shrieking through the rigging, the waves pounding against the hull of poor old "Möwe", the clunking of the self-steering when the wheel turned. But most of all the noise of a man shouting. Susie soon understood the problem. "Möwe"'s alternator had broken and the spare one did not fit, at all, Hans was desperate. "Where did you get this piece of shit," Susie peeked out of her bunk to the open engine compartment where Poldi was berating her poor husband, flushed with anger.

No electric power meant no communication, no self-steering and lights, even flushing the electric toilet became impossible. "Back to hand steering and a bucket," Hans thought, but did not say that aloud to not further spook his terrified wife. The first week of the crossing had been hell for the elderly German sailors. "Möwe" had been pounded by the oncoming waves as high as seven meters. They seemed to make slow progress, it simply had been a terrifying journey so far. Poldi behaved like Captain Bligh, bossing them around and giving them no peace. What a mistake it had been to take him on board, the elderly couple whispered to each other. They could not turn around now, they were too far away from the Canaries, but the journey would be even more uncomfortable without electricity. If only the weather would improve a bit.

Thea

"And how are you this morning, darling?" They had moved from "my dear" to "darling" within a few days, and Hanna involuntarily blushed and looked around when she heard Peter's voice through the satphone. But nobody was listening in. Peter Taylor of Pogo 40 "Crazy" did not have to ask where she was as they were in the same group in the daily HF radio sched and noted down each other's and the rest of the group's position every day. Rally Control's tracker was fastened to the back of the boat but "Thea" rarely had internet, the mail program was playing up as in so many other boats. The HF roll call was a great way of hearing news of other boats and exchanging weather information. After the sched there was the Aussie net run by Dania's Steve which was good fun to listen to.

Hanna on "Thea" was talking to Peter on the satphone. They had fallen into the routine of a daily phone call around 5pm to talk about each other's day. They decided to avoid the SSB as the whole fleet could listen in on what they were saying. And although their chat was harmless it still felt more private on the phone. "What's happening your end, gorgeous," his lovely British accent somehow sounded stronger through the phone. "We are really close to "Gdynia", too close for comfort," Hanna told her friend. "After what he did to you at the start I am worried he might hit me, so we ae playing cat and mouse." Pavel clearly enjoyed sailing very close behind the Norwegian Swan, trying to make his opponent nervous.

They exchanged some gossip. On Australian boat "Nipper", skipper Joe had decided he needed to go for a wind surf in the middle of the Atlantic, naked of course. So in a short wind lull the board was launched and photos of the event posted to the whole fleet. Others went for a swim midway or flew kites of the back of the boat. It was a long journey, time seemed to stand still.

Dania

However, despite the mishaps of some participants most of the CAR fleet had a peaceful crossing after the first few windy days. On day eight the crew of "Dania" felt totally in tune with their boat and the ocean.

Carla wrote in her diary": Quiet night at good speeds, beam reaching on a steady course. One reef and No 3 headsail. All are in good spirits though Frankie has a cold. We shake the reef out and unfurl the big genoa. I phone German weather router Sven on the satphone to hear about the approaching low. He says it can't be avoided and will produce lulls, a difficult few days ahead. Kids get history audio CDs, very interesting. Frankie and I bake banana bread and beer bread, pancakes for lunch. We play cards, she wins. Kids watch "Treasure Buddies". In the afternoon the kids start to fight, Leif wants to steer, Frankie gets competitive. We try to have a buffet dinner with our new beer bread but a rain squall arrives and all goes pear shaped, food on the cockpit floor this time, sigh. Steve earlier talked to Henk from "Andante", they are having all sorts of trouble after a knock down, poor Kirsten. We are going into the night with full main and No 3. For the midnight watch the boat is going like a train, more than 10 knots, it feels too fast, rounds up, the autopilot can't cope. Steve and I furl headsail in and put engine on for charge, nobody sleeps a lot that night. In Steve's early watch at dawn we reef and unfurl the jib, better balance." The fleet was now well spread out with most boats taking the middle route while some ambitious sailed further north and some cautious skippers tried the butter melting southern route.

“Peter,” Hanna sobbed into her satphone, Peter got a real fright when he heard her distress. “I have lost Elsbeth, she fell overboard last night. You would not believe what this tosser Urs did on his watch,” she cried. “He was in the cockpit by himself around 1 am, I was sending emails down below via HF when a squall came through. He could not hear the wind noise because of his noise cancelling headphones and did not watch the wind angle instrument, so when it started gusting over 30 the self-steering conked out, the boat gybed and the preventer broke. We then rounded up, it was mayhem. Elsbeth came out of the companionway without her harness to help, but Urs by then had put the autopilot on standby and gybed the boat back. It was such a crash gybe Elsbeth was flung over the side by the main sheet. It was the worst moment of my life, I can still see her go over the rail in slow motion. I shot a white flare so we could see her in the water, and the only good thing was that Pavel was so close behind us he managed to pick her up, it was a miracle. I have spoken to Elsbeth and she will sail the rest of the trip on “Gdynia”, the sea state is too rough to try a transfer. How could this have happened to me, it’s so unprofessional!”

Peter tried to calm Hanna down, she was beside herself. It took a while before she could continue her account. She eventually sighed: “Apart from the Elsbeth thing we were so lucky “Thea” is a Swan and the boom and its fitting are oversized, we could have easily broken something major. You should have seen the mess down below, and one of the Germans fell out of his bunk and hit his head, but seems ok now. The Germans were great in all this, I will be allright without Elsbeth I think. But I will not leave this idiot in the cockpit by himself again!” Peter was very sympathetic and said all the right things so when Hanna eventually hung up she felt much better.

Elsbeth had come to terms with sailing on Pavel's boat after the initial shock of falling into the water and the utmost relief when she was picked up so soon. She had been terrified in the black sea, fearing for her life. Without a locator beacon it was very hard for Hanna to find her in the big seas, Elsbeth knew that, and without a life vest she could not swim very long. She had smiled sheepishly at Pavel when she had slowly climbed up "Gdynia"s bathing ladder, utterly exhausted. What would he think of her, what a completely stupid thing to happen? But to her surprise he smiled back and handed her a huge towel and a hot tea, even with rum. She had told him about the gybes. and he had been understanding and really nice. And he was incredibly good-looking, Elsbeth had to admit to herself. Maybe the rest of the trip would not be so bad after all.

At this half way point of the rally most competitors were sailing along fairly settled and skippers were really interested in how they were doing in their group and overall. Boats with internet were checking the tracker, other compared positions. Hanna knew her CAR-rival Pavel would get time redress for picking up Elsbeth, it would be a close race. Not that it really mattered, the main thing was that Elsbeth was safe. It was strange, though, that she had not heard from Elsbeth in a few days, hopefully she was ok.

Chapter 11

Chinese Strife

"Mayday, mayday, mayday, this is yacht Saiche!" "Elbe" skipper Sven jumped up from the chart table where he had been resting his head for a quick power nap. It had been a difficult night on the Northern route, squalls up to 35 knots with plenty of headsail changes and reefing of the mainsail to keep the crew busy. The cruisers would not bother about the last half knot of boat speed but Sven needed to get to St Lucia first. Now in the early light somebody was in trouble, nearby. Sven grabbed the VHF and replied "Yacht Saiche, this is Elbe, Elbe, Elbe, can you hear me?" "I can hear you, Sven," sounded the exhausted voice of his old school friend Soren Meyer through the VHF. "What is the matter, mate, how can we help?" Soren was brief: "Saiche" had lost its rudder. The titanium stock had broken, whether through a wrong design or material fatigue, who knew, they had tried an emergency set up with two poles, with drogues, but the boat just would not settle and sail in a straight line. Or any line at all. "Modern boats, who needs them, dad's old long keeler would have driven like on tracks," Soren tried to make light of it but to his close friend he sounded very disheartened.

"We are around 15 miles behind you, just two hours, we will come and help you," Sven didn't hesitate. "Get the life raft ready, if you have to abandon ship it will be easier to transfer you in the raft." Completely exhausted, Soren looked around the cabin of the Chinese racer. The chaos was unbelievable, there was freeze dried food bags and tins on the floor from when a cupboard had opened. The two Chinese women were cowering in one corner of the saloon, embracing each other. Non-sailors, who were on the boat solely to cook and clean, they had been really brave and not uttered a sound, but Soren could see the fear in their tired faces. The Asian skipper and crew had been completely hopeless after the rudder fell out, lack of experience. He had just about killed himself getting some sort of emergency steering working, but to no avail. Bone tired Soren climbed into the cockpit and started to give orders to get the life raft ready.

Möwe

"If he complains about the cold food one more time I will kill him!" Flushed red with anger Susie stood in front of her cold stove and looked into her warm fridge to see whether there was anything left to use. It had come as a real surprise to her how much one relies on power on a boat, nothing worked without it. She had not been able to even use her gas cooker because the solenoid on-switch did not work without electricity. It was getting harder and harder to assemble anything eatable as the supplies of fresh fruit and vege dwindled. But Poldi's thrice-daily rages about the food were completely out of order, it was not as if she wasn't trying. They all had lost a few kilos already and maybe ten days to go.

Dania

Most boats were luckier than the poor Germans. On day 12 Carla noted the uneventful events of the day: "Rain. Nate spots a huge school of dolphins. Kids stay in their pyjamas, why not. Frankie feels much better, has warm raspberries and hot cocoa for breakfast. Fresh supplies dwindle, the last kiwis, a few bananas and apples left. A possible shortage of milk and tea looming, those English habits. Josh and Nate love hot beverages. It is grey with squalls and thunderstorms as expected as we spoke to the weather man yesterday. 1200 miles to go, around seven days which would get us in around Dec 17, with luck! Huge thunderstorm late morning, torrential rain and strong winds. Nate and Josh are outside when a huge wave goes over the boat and into the cockpit. We lose one cushion and Josh's life vest inflates. It is a total lockdown below with temperatures like a sauna, it lasts 1 ½ hours. The boys are drenched. Steve hears on the SSB that "Skyelark" is through it. We turn the engine on at 12.15, crank the fans on and write emails to Hamburg and our friends. Chicken stir-fry for dinner. Most amazing fiery sunset. Josh hears a whale blowing next to the boat. A quiet night."

"Carla, darling, get up quickly!" Steve was leaning over her, it was light already. Carla automatically looked at her watch, it was 6am. "What is it, are we all right?" Carla was wide awake in a second. "Yes, no problems, but we have to stand by and help the Chinese boat and another boat called "Elbe", they are doing a crew transfer with a life raft. They must have come down from a more northern route in the last few days. The Chinese have lost their rudder. We are the closest boat, they have been trying for hours, the first raft drifted away, they are now going to try with a second raft." Donning oilskins and life vest Carla soon climbed into the back cockpit and peered to port. Nathan and Josh stood in the front cockpit. Half a mile away two boats were swaying in the huge waves, dangerously close. Sails were down, Carla could see water coming out of the Hanseatic "Elbe's" exhaust so she had the engine on. "Dania"'s motor was also running and Nathan and Josh were putting the sails away.

Carla looked on helplessly as the two other boats tried to establish a rope connection without colliding, letting a fender with a rope drift from "Saiche" to "Elbe" behind her. "What are they trying to do here, they are not getting it across, the waves are too high, the fender doesn't drift?" quizzically she turned to Steve. "A tow rope would not be much use anyway I think, the Hanseatic can't tow a similar sized boat across the Atlantic. Looks like those two guys are getting the second raft ready now but they are very slow. Where is the rest of the crew? And surely one raft can't be big enough for all of them?"

"Man, just pull yourself together and pay attention to what I say, we almost got the line across," Soren was at breaking point, berating his crew unfairly, struggling through every skipper's worst nightmare. Without steerage the boat was being tossed about by the massive waves. "Saiche" was in danger of being rolled. Their attempt of establishing a line connection had failed, quite predictably. But Soren could not think straight any longer, he was too exhausted. "Don't worry about the fender, let's go for the second raft. Shu-Yi, give Huan a hand, quick, but hold on to something while you lift it! And tie the end of the release onto the middle cleat." The two men were struggling under the heavy load of the raft. "Open the gate to leeward, push it through there, good, let me pull the release!" A huge wave hit "Saiche"'s hull, the boat heeled over heavily, and one of the two crew man lost his footing and almost went over with the raft. But his colleague grabbed him by the arm and pulled him back. The raft hit the water, and with a last, superhuman effort Soren started to pull meter after meter of the release rope, until finally the white container burst open and the orange raft inflated. "Get the grab bags and some extra water and call everybody up," Soren yelled over the cacophonic noise of the wind and waves.

Steve looked through his binoculars. "They are throwing the raft over the side and pulling the quick release, let's hope the raft's line holds this time." Steve turned the big wheel, steering "Dania" well clear of the other two boats. "The raft is alongside now, they are starting to get the crew in," Carla exclaimed. "One, two, three, it looks like there are eight at least, the raft doesn't look big enough for them." She could make out that a tall man with a ponytail, maybe the skipper, was the last to climb over the rail into the raft, a grab bag over his shoulder. "Let's hope "Elbe" can pick them up, but we are going closer, just in case," Steve said. Carla knew that if necessary they had to take the other sailors onto "Dania" for the rest of the trip, law of the sea, that's what you did. But how difficult that would be in terms of the logistics, sleeping, food etc.

Chapter 12

The Rescue

"Come up, all of you," Soren had shouted into the companionway after securing the raft to the boat. But nothing happened, what were they doing? He stuck his head into the companionway. "What's the matter, do you need a special invitation, come on, everybody. We could go turtle any minute!" Shu-Yi, the most competent of the novice crew looked at him pleadingly. "It is the boss, he doesn't want to move, we don't know what to do!" Soren hopped down the companionway ladder and started shaking the immobile figure of his Chinese skipper in the port bunk. "Get up you idiot, we are abandoning ship, do you want to go down with her." The man stirred and slowly sat upright, avoiding Soren's eyes. Soren checked on the women, they seemed a bit less scared now that they knew they would leave the boat. "All right everybody, you know the drill, let's count through the assigned crew numbers, everybody check their crotch strap is tight and then I will call one number after the other on deck. It will not be easy to get in the raft, we have to time the jump between waves."

Soren climbed back out into the cockpit and pulled the wildly rocking life raft close. The boat's high freeboard let the raft seem meters away. Shu-Yi and Huan were standing by, Soren called down: "Number 1, go!" The boat heeled heavily again, water rushed into the cockpit on starboard. With difficulty one of the men climbed out into the cockpit and positioned himself at the leeward gate. Looking down, he decided to sit down in the gate and lower himself into the raft entrance. Relieved Soren turned and yelled "No 2!" One by one the crew managed to get into the raft. Soren didn't want to think about how crowded it would be in the four man raft with eight people. He had wanted two six man rafts but his request had been refused by the yard. The two women came up one after the other and both looked utterly terrified, gauging the jump into the small entrance of the orange float hopping in the foaming water. But in the end they made it.

Going down below was almost too much for the bone-weary skipper. With a last effort Soren grabbed the wallet with the ships papers, looked around a final time and finally lowered his long legs into the raft, on top of the other bodies. He stayed in the raft entrance and let the whole trigger rope run through into the water to give the other boat a chance to pick it up.

The orange raft with its little tent was free now, being tossed about madly in the big seas. Expertly "Elbe" with all crew on deck in life jackets and with harnesses on manoeuvred close to the raft, and a crew man managed to pick up the raft's line with a boat hook on the third attempt. "They have them, thank god," Steve looked relieved. "They are helping the crew out of the raft, look, they are lifting the women up just like dolls, I have met them in the supermarket," Carla said. The wind had eased a bit and they were now so close that Carla could make out the frightened, frozen faces. Steve was talking into the cockpit VHF. "Elbe, Elbe, Elbe, this is Dania, over." "Dania, this is Elbe, we are all good now, what a nightmare. We might need a bit of food on the way, but won't try a transfer in these conditions, will talk to you later, thanks for standing by, over."

On "Möwe" things were grim. Susie had woken up at dawn on day 14 feeling utterly miserable. This nightmare just wasn't ending. They had not been in contact with rally control or others for days and days and Susie felt very alone. She peeked over her lee cloth to the other saloon bunk, Hans looked grey and ill, but was still asleep.

“Let’s hope he does not get a heart attack or stroke, that’s all we need now,” Susie thought. “Hey lazybones down there, anything to eat, I am working up here you know?” As if they did nothing, she thought outraged, both had to stand their four-hour watch and hand-steer as the auto pilot did not work any longer. Susie’s arms felt like jelly, the steering was really hard. Hans and her now tried to stay away from Poldi as much as they could.

But the Austrian needed constant feeding, how much the man could eat, it was unbelievable. They were on small rations now but Poldi ate a double portion each meal, Susie was not sure the provisions would last. She had bought plenty of flour after the enlightening food seminar in Las Palmas, and she now could bake bread. Hans had disconnected the electric safety switch and they were firing oven and stove with good old-fashioned matches now, thank god. Slowly she lifted herself out of her bunk and put a pre-prepared bread tin with dough in the oven. Poldi from Salzburg liked his bread fresh and warm, she had found that out the hard way.

There had been an article in Yacht magazine recently, she remembered, about the psychology of crews, the conflicts and confrontations, sometimes ending in violence and murder. She felt like violence and murder when Poldi was particularly nasty, especially to poor Hans. The man was a psychopath, she thought, she could not even look at him any longer when she passed him the food. “I will not ever go sailing again when this is over,” she promised herself and fingered the family photo of the children out of its plastic cover. They were all that kept her going, and darling Hans, who she would support until the end.

Hanna on “Thea” had minor problems in comparison, but crew problems nevertheless. The Swiss sailor Urs had turned out not to be a sailor at all. He might have sailed dinghies on Lake Geneva, but had no idea of seamanship on a yacht. That in itself should not have been a problem, everybody who wants to can learn the ropes, and they had enough experience on board to be safe. But Urs acted as if he had booked a five-start cruise, could not be trusted with any boat work and was demanding as a four-year old. Hanna almost wondered whether he was trying to sabotage her easy crossing. The German charter guests on the other hand were good-humoured, but Hanna did not want their experience of a life time spoiled by an ill-mannered outsider. “Only four days to go,” she thought staring at her chart. “I just need to keep him out of the cockpit. Maybe somebody can play chess with him, he was boasting about his proficiency last night.”

Chapter 13

The Finish

Day 17, the sun rose and the arriving boats saw the hills of St. Lucia to their left, in a morning haze, just like that. "Dania's" little crew was up at 5am, only a few miles to go now. Leif sat on the deck and looked across at the land, Frankie chatted happily in the cockpit. Carla took photos and Steve spoke to fellow Australian Ian from "Sundancer II" to find out whether he needed assistance to get into port as his engine had stopped working, but Ian, the old racer, crossed the finish line under sail just ahead. A yacht with a big CAR flag was anchored in the bay and took down the finish times. It was sunny, hot, tropical smells wafted across from the land. They had arrived, it was unbelievable how completely normal this felt. In 17 hair-raising days "Dania" had trucked across the Atlantic. She had done them proud and the time at sea had passed so fast. It had been great!

"Hey, man, don't work so hard, you are going to have a heart attack, man, relax!" The friendly guy sent as marina welcome committee handed Steve a rum punch. The kids were hopping around the deck. "Who can you spot, who is here yet." Even at 5am it certainly was a Caribbean atmosphere, the rum punch tasted delicious. Steve and Carla hugged. They were there, in the Caribbean!

More and more boats arrived, it was a happy, even elated atmosphere in Rodney Bay Marina. The entry formality in the marina office took a while, there were three stations with officials and endless forms to fill in for customs, harbour control and police, but soon the "Dania" family was exploring the shops and catching up with a few other families. Many were still out there at sea, to the May family's great surprise they had been faster than most.

Next morning Carla and Steve and the kids were enjoying smoothies and eggs and bacon for breakfast in the popular breakfast spot Café Ola, with a tired all-girl crew drinking beer at the table next to them celebrating their arrival. "Have you heard about the Germans, that arrogant lawyer, their mast broke three days before reaching St Lucia and they ordered a tug boat to get them in," a friend leant over from the next table. "No, really, poor Sabine and the little boys, she was so worried ahead of the trip. What bad luck." Carla commented.

The arrival of "Hanseatic" drew a big crowd midday. The 60-footer moored effortlessly amongst the super yachts with people cheering and blowing horns. The deck was crowded, not a crew of twelve but twenty people were standing and waving. After they had picked up the "Saiche" crew from their stricken boat it had been a long hard slog for the German boat with that many people on the boat. Food had run low soon, and after the mainsail halyard broke on day 15 they had a very slow trip the rest of the way to St Lucia. But now they were all here, and there were happy and relieved faces all around.

Hanna also had a huge smile on her face. She was motoring "Thea" through the narrow channel leading into the marina basin, sniffing the Caribbean air and looking at the colourful local fishing boats stacked on a ramp to the left, when her crew suddenly gesticulated and yelled from the foredeck. "Faster Hanna, faster, throttle forward!" Hanna pushed the lever down instantly and turned around to see the big Hanse trying to overtake her here in the tight channel. "You are an idiot, Pavel, you are dangerous, I will report you," she yelled at her nemesis, not that that would make any difference to the nasty brute, she thought. "Thea" was charging ahead, Hanna did not let "Gdynia" through, not here, not ever, she had finished first. Peter was standing on the dock taking their lines, and without hesitation Hanna threw herself into his arms. "Well done, babes," he grinned from ear to ear and swiftly kissed her, in front of everybody. Hanna did not care one bit about what people were thinking.

CAR land life kick started again as more and more boats arrived. Happy hour drinks, provisioning, some sightseeing, the rally gang soon settled into a slower, Caribbean style routine.

The little Bavaria was one of the last boats to arrive. News had somehow seeped through that the German yacht was being towed and was due in around 2am. From 1am onward a little group of friends gathered on an outside pontoon where "Möwe" could dock without engine power. Carla and Steve were sitting there, Germans Kerstin and Robert from "Trinity" and a few other German sailors. People were sipping rum punches and chatting. At 2.40 finally a small shadow drifted toward them, and Susie threw the fore line in a heap onto the dock. She sat down on the front hatch and buried her head in her hands. Quickly her girlfriends jumped on board and embraced her. How thin she looked, just awful! Once the boat was safely tied up Steve handed Hans a glass of straight rum and sat him down in the cockpit. The poor people, what had they been through.

Carla peered into the dark cabin of the small boat. "Who is that on the bunk, what happened to him?" Startled she turned to Hans. "That is our last-minute crew member Poldi, he fell over," Hans was as white as a sheet and clearly exhausted. "He needs an ambulance I think." "How did it happen, a freak wave? " Hans seemed fairly uninterested in Poldi's state of health. "Yeah, a wave I think, he hit his head and has been mainly unconscious for a few days."

Somebody was already on the phone to rally control to organise medical help, and soon Poldi was carried down the dock on a stretcher. Carla organised cold pizza and some cheese to nibble on while Hans and Susie slowly recounted their ordeal. Poldi didn't get much of a mention in the saga.

Chapter 14

St Lucia

"I would rank these three out of ten," Carla sighed towelling herself off. The Rodney Bay marina showers only had hot water for a very short time in the morning. That did not matter to her that much, as she was an early riser. But what did matter was the hooker she had surprised behind one shower curtain with a swarmy looking guy. They had both dashed out when Carla had pulled the curtain aside, she was just glad she did not have Frankie with her. Carla longingly thought of her power shower back at home in Sydney.

Carla bumped into rally employee Susan and told her about the shower scene. "The hooker problem is really hard to control," Susan sighed, "they are also on the docks at night despite the security guards, but it is also the sailors' fault, they are the ones who hire them."

Distraction was at hand soon enough, though. The fresh food market lured with exotic produce, for instance yellow and orange super spicy bell peppers and beautiful fruit. A kids' birthday party was planned on the lawn early afternoon. Days after their arrival Carla felt fully recovered from the crossing and thoroughly enjoyed the Caribbean atmosphere. Life was easy. Also the party schedule had restarted. Rally drinks were followed by the famous Gros Islet Jump Up on Friday night. "Don't stay past eight with the kids, it can get rowdy," somebody recommended, advice Steve and Carla planned to follow.

Thumping music, unfortunately not reggae, greeted them walking down the Gros Islet high street. Women were grilling meat and skewers on outside barbecues while rasta guys served rum punch out of huge plastic bottles. The whole town was on the street, it was the locals' party and they did not mind the visitors joining in, although each stuck to their own.

"Mum, can I have one of them," Leif pleaded with Carla, pointing at a young local who was making locusts out of leaves. "Sure, darling, here, give him a few EC dollars," Carla smiled. At this time of the night it certainly felt completely safe here on the street.

Two hours later it was a slightly different story. "How stupid am I, I shouldn't have gone in here," Hanna looked around in a light panic. She had been to the Jump Up before and knew there could be fist fights and muggings later in the night. But it was still only 9pm and she had not hesitated when the street barman whose jerry can had run out of rum punch had waved her toward a house entrance and signalled her he had more punch there. She had lost Peter who had said he needed something to eat and was nowhere to be seen now.

Hanna's eyes took a while to adjust to the darkness in the house, a crowd of people was in here, lots of loud voices, music thumping, but the punch guy had disappeared. Hanna hesitated and felt for her wallet as a tall guy brushed past her. This corridor was not the place to be, she moved further into the house, curious to see how these people lived but feeling slightly guilty about it. Through the doorway she peeked into what might be a living room, there was a sofa and an armchair, a frayed carpet but little else. Almost thirty people were in the room, drinking and talking. There was so much smoke from the barbecues on the street and the joints that her eyes were burning. Not really her scene, and she was the only white person here she suddenly realised.

"Hey, Miss, can I help you?" Oh, no, it was the toothless guy from the vegetable stall at the market that had pestered her this morning about buying some more mangos. In the end she had bought some passion fruit from him that she didn't want, but took because he was so persistent. She knew it was ridiculous, but she found him creepy.

Maybe he was doped to his eyeballs, or he was just trying to be friendly and make a living out of the boatie tourists. Hanna realized she had no idea about these people even after coming here for years. She put on what she thought was a friendly grin, With "I'm ok, thanks," she turned around to leave but he grabbed her shoulder. She tried to shake the guy off and ran into a tall figure blocking her way. Now she was in full panic, trying to push past the newcomer. "Babes, it's me," Peter folded her into his arms and gave her a kiss. "Let's get out of here, what are you doing, I saw you disappear through the door and followed you." Hanna could have cried she was so relieved, why had she not waited for him in the first place.

"What's he doing over there, look!" Hanna and Peter were still thirty meters away from the petrol station on the road back to the marina. A woman was singing karaoke with all her heart and in a beautiful voice, but next to her a shady looking local guy was handing Pavel a brown envelope. "That looks like drugs, what an idiot, if he gets caught he will end up in a Caribbean prison. Not a nice place I am sure." Peter took Hanna's hand and they slowly followed the future inmate, keeping a distance. The shortcut to the boats on the family dock was a floating pontoon next to the Captain's Table restaurant. Another couple was waiting and Pavel pulled the pontoon toward them all. Hanna and Peter jumped on last minute. "This ferry is full, no room for you," the Pole sneered, dropping the pull rope and starting to push and shove the surprised Hanna. She lost her balance and went straight in the water. "You seem to have a bad memory, sunshine, remember this one?" Peter showed Pavel his fist and decked the aggressor. In one swift move Peter snatched the envelope out of Pavel's shirt pocket and emptied its content out into the water. He watched thirty small pills floating to the bottom of the sea.

Chapter 15

Post Rally Fun

"Pull, pull harder," the rally kids were hanging at the end of a fat rope and, with the help of some adults, were trying to pull their opponents over the line in a tug of war. Their disadvantage of pulling up the beach while the others were pulling toward the water was compensated by Nathan and some other beefy guys on their side. "We did it, we won," Frankie shouted toward her mother. "Next is the Limbo, I can do that!" The CAR Olympics at Spinnakers beach bar were in full swing.

Looking at the old racing photos on the way to the toilet, Carla noticed the pony-tailed skipper of "Saiche" and another Germanic looking guy sitting at the bar with a beer. In an impulse she went over to them. "Hi guys, that was a well-conducted rescue, you should be proud. What was it like with so many people on the boat?" "Thanks, sweetheart," Mr Ponytail said smiling. It made him look like a little boy. Carla suddenly recognized him from their collision on the pontoon in Las Palmas. "It certainly was a test for crew and boat," the other, more serious guy said. He was the skipper of "Elbe" Carla realised. "A lot of hot-bunking and pasta with ketchup. We couldn't have gone much longer. Thanks for handing over a care packet after the rescue. The biscuits and chocolate were very popular." Carla couldn't help herself. "Any idea yet what happened to your rudder?" she asked the "Saiche" skipper. "No, not at all. But we will soon find out I hope," he answered ominously. Carla left it at that and returned to the action on the beach. Nathan was just winning the competition for their team with an outstanding striptease, no problem for a former Royal Marine.

After a full-on fun day at the beach Leif steered the family dinghy safely back through the passage to the marina. Their big lunch at Spinnakers meant it was just going to be a light snack and off to bed for the kids, while the adults were planning to sip a drink in somebody's cockpit, bliss!

As more and more boats arrived and the euphoria of getting across safely was slowly subsiding gossip was rampant. People heard rumours in the marina office, on the VHF or in the shower. There were three main topics. What had happened to the Chinese boat's rudder and should the boat have been abandoned, how had Poldi sustained his head injury, and would "Crazy" win the rally by handicap. There were also rumours circulating about the arrogant German lawyer's lost rig and attempts to get his boat back on track to sail the Northwest Passage. "Northwest Passage, what does he want to do that for? How about exploring the Caribbean first, people spend years enjoying this here?" Australian Basil could not believe the German's apparent contempt for the beautiful and exotic surroundings.

Authorities and rally control started asking questions about some of the mid-ocean incidents. The happy hour drinks were even louder than normal, the pool bar was buzzing. Due to the strong winds at the beginning and a few ill-prepared participants there had been more than usual damage to the boats. Fortunately nobody in the fleet was seriously hurt apart from Poldi who they heard was on the mend.

The criminal inquiry into Poldi's accident bore no firm result. He did not remember what had happened, and both Hans and Susie's explanations remained somehow vague, but were conclusive and matched. So the file was closed. Carla approached Susie resting on a sun lounger at the pool with a book. "Good to see you with a bit of colour, Susie, how are you feeling?" Susie looked up startled. "Oh, it's you Carla, I was a million miles away. Thanks for asking, I am much better. And tomorrow my daughter and the children will arrive, I can't wait to see them. And guess what, our son-in-law will not come out now, but save his holiday and help sail the boat from

Antigua via Bermuda back home in April. So Hans and I will enjoy a few months here in the Caribbean and I won't have to worry about another ocean crossing." "That is such a great result, I am so pleased," Carla smiled. "Much better than the Kellermanns, they are putting their boat on a freighter back to Europe, somebody said Sabine and the children have already left, would you believe it, before Christmas, she must just have enough!" "I know the feeling, but a good shower and a few rum punches later I changed my mind," Susie grinned. Carla was relieved, no permanent damage done, her friend was evidently not still traumatised from the horrific crossing.

Peter, who else, eventually found out about "Saiche". He told Hanna: "The Chinese owner has organised an ocean going tug from Antigua to go out and search for the boat, its EPIRB is still signalling its position, they have a fair chance of finding it. Hugely costly, though. I wonder why they bother."

The Toga party was the last big hurrah of the rally events, the prize giving a day later was a more formal affair and some of the boats had already left. Wrapped in white sheets the fleet piled into maxi taxis and headed for a night club near Pidgeon Island. "Mama, this is very dark here," Frankie piped grabbing Carla's hand. "Look, darling, over there are all the children, where the light is in front of the stage." The CAR kids soon hopped to the live band's beats while the adults enjoyed a drink and a chat.

Carla had been contacted by her old editor about the drama with the Chinese entry. He had seen a newswire report and had asked her to fill in some details and write a short news story. Happy to keep her name in the game, Carla had started to ask around at the party. She had tried the two crewmen that were standing near the bar. The other "Saiche" crew were obviously enjoying their hotel or had already flown home. "How is it going, have you recovered from the ordeal," she smiled at them, but got only a nod and a stare back from one, the other didn't even move a muscle. Frustrated, Carla turned away and headed in the other direction. To her surprise she spotted the two Chinese women she had met in the super market. Why were they still here? "Hello, nice to see you, how are you feeling?" she enquired and looked at the younger one encouragingly, the one that had spoken to her in the supermarket. Carefully looking around first the woman slowly answered: "Much better, thank you." Carla probed further: "Why are you still here, can't you go home, are you still needed?" The women made sure nobody was listening in and then said: "Boat is being rescued, we have to wait with skipper in house, cook and wash for him. Not long now we hope." Carla got really interested. She smiled at the women and asked: "I would like to interview your boss. Where can I find him, is he here." But the younger woman just shook her head and walked away.

After an hour of socialising Carla had enough, she felt talked out and a bit weary, and started walking toward the water. To the right a path opened up, winding up a hill, possibly toward Pidgeon Island, the iconic St Lucia headland that was no island any longer. Carla climbed higher and higher in the hope of getting a good view of the marina. She had her camera with her as always. Here, a gap in the trees! Carla steadied her camera on a tree branch to take a shot without camera shake. She looked through the viewfinder of her SLR taking in the whole bay, a few anchored boats in the fore ground, the marina in the back.

When she fell forward into the darkness she at first couldn't believe it, it seemed like a scene out of a movie. Somebody had pushed her, as simple as that, she was flying. A second later instinct set in, windmill-style she flung her arms around to try and hold on to something, ouch, she had landed hard, was sliding fast, branches scratching her face and arms. She tried to grab the ground vegetation but kept on sliding, belly down. Suddenly a jolt, the fall was stopped. Her camera strap had caught around a tree branch.

Carla tried to calm her breath and cried a bit, which helped, but her whole body was hurting. Why was her first thought of Frodo Baggins hanging off the edge of the fires of Mount Doom. Where did that come from? Oh, they had taken the kids to watch "The Hobbit" in St Lucia the day before, Frodo appeared in one of the opening scenes. This could also be a scene out of a Hitchcock movie. But where was Cary Grant? "Carla, get a grip on yourself," she thought and assessed her situation with her eyes adjusting to the darkness. She was stuck in the dense cliff side vegetation, hanging off a thin strap. Maybe she could get herself into a safer position, she wondered. But the way the camera was tightly strapped to her body by her own weight meant she could hardly move. How long would it take Steve or the kids to notice she was missing? And would he not assume she had gone back to the boat? But without telling him first, not likely.

Carla turned her head and saw a massive rock to her right. Thank god she had not hit that, she would have broken bones or worse. Maybe she could pull herself up on that. She reached out and grabbed the tip of the rock with her right hand, she could comfortably reach it, good. The camera strap was jammed under her left arm, so to get across to the rock Carla had to pull her arm out of the strap. She found some foot support, got on her toes and tried to free her arm while lunging to the right. Carla had sweat trickling into her eyes by now. One, two, three, she was hanging off the rock with both arms. Without the camera, of course, but that was a problem for day light. Pulling up and wedging her knees into rock crevices Carla managed to climb onto the rock. This was much better. But she couldn't get any further up the cliff without help. She started to shout, "help, help" in regular intervals. It felt like forever, but after only a few minutes somebody answered from above. Soon Steve in a climbing harness with a rope attached landed on her rock and looked at her very concerned. "Darling! How did you get down here, a big fall, are you all right, hurt anywhere?"

Soon Carla was sitting on a wooden bench sipping a rum punch and inspecting her wounds. People had moved on after the initial excitement and Steve was just organising a taxi. She would tell him all about the push when they were back on “Dania” and the kids in their bunks. Who wanted to harm her here, had she done anything to induce such an attack? Had she taken a photo of something secret? Or had it just been a misguided prank?

Chapter 16

Christmas in Marigot Bay

The prize giving behind them, on Dec 23 the rally family boats left Rodney Bay to celebrate Christmas together. "What a shame, it is only 12 miles of sailing," Steve sighed, but Carla was quietly relieved Marigot Bay was just a short sail around the corner. She was still feeling fragile after her fall and was not sure what it meant. Leaving Rodney Bay was probably a good thing.

Hanna eased the main halyard, the mainsail folding almost by itself into the lazy jacks, she just had to put a few ties around the sail. "How easy it is to sail with somebody that knows what he is doing and that you can trust completely," she thought, smiling back toward the cockpit where Peter was steering "Thea" expertly toward the mooring field in Marigot Bay.

As their romance had accelerated and felt really comfortable, Hanna and Peter had decided to leave Peter's brothers with the boys' boat in St Lucia to supervise some repairs and keep on partying, while the "two love birds" as Nick called them, sailed "Thea" south for ten days before the next charter load arrived for Hanna. Her German guests had been extremely complimentary about a perfect crossing, while the annoying Urs to her surprise had jumped ship to Pavel minutes after "Gdynia" arrived in Rodney Bay. "Why didn't he sail with them in the first place if he is such good friends with Pavel," Hanna mused.

She had been extremely surprised to see Elsbeth and Pavel openly kissing, she had not seen a lot of Elsbeth after the close finish. Elsbeth had stayed on the Polish boat, and Hanna felt slightly betrayed. It had been right, obviously, that Pavel and also Sven from "Elbe" had gotten redress for rescuing people and thus bettered their corrected time, but Hanna was silently annoyed that Pavel had beaten her this way, her own fault though, if she was honest.

Described by novelist James A Michener as the "most beautiful bay in the Caribbean" Marigot Bay even now is a cruiser's dream with its rows of palm trees and long sand spit. The recently built resort with its boutiques, shops and accommodation in grey-slatted wooden buildings was sitting well in its surroundings. The marina offered service facilities to fit every type of boat. But the CAR families were not here to pamper their boats, they were here to celebrate.

Carla did not want to anchor, she announced firmly while motoring in, she wanted easy access to the shore. After their great achievement and Carla's hard work during the crossing Steve did not mind paying for a berth for a few nights. The dock master led them into the second berth in, next to a stunning wooden Super Yacht.

That night the Mays had dinner at the Rainbow Hideaway restaurant on a voucher they had won in the rally. When they pulled up in their dinghy at 6.30 for an early dinner only one other table was occupied. "The Kellermanns! Somebody had said they had left," Carla exclaimed and walked over to say hello to Sabine. Thomas Kellermann looked up annoyed when Carla approached the table, but Sabine smiled and beckoned Carla to sit in a free chair next to Leon and Markus. "Good to see you guys," Carla said, "Are you staying in a hotel here, I haven't seen your boat?" "No, our boat is on a freighter heading home, we are on this big wooden boat over there, Thomas has chartered it for the Christmas period." Sabine said slightly sheepish. Glancing over to the Super Yacht Carla couldn't hide her surprise: "Amazing, wow, we are right next to it, what is it like, you must give us a tour tomorrow! But I'll leave you to your meal now."

The Island tour on Christmas Eve through banana plantations and up and down steep hills was extremely interesting and also great fun.

The family crews of "Dania" and "Chili Cat" were singing Christmas carols while watching make-shift butchers on the roadside cutting off big chunks of meat for a Christmas roast, the driver dodging school girls with white ribbons in their hair walking home. The children loved the exhilarating zip-lining through the jungle while parents found the mud-bath at the end of their trip very relaxing. Tired and happy the gang watched the colourful scenery. The bus was driving through the Piton town Soufriere when Steve pointed to the left. "Carla, is that not the unfriendly German?" Thomas Kellermann stood on the side of the road talking to a local guy in a suit. "I wonder what he is up to?"

Christmas Day on the sand spit met everybody's expectations of a happy Christmas celebration in the Caribbean. Everybody had brought food and drinks, the adults were sipping champagne while the kids were swinging off a rope over the water and later looking for treasure on the sea wall. The sailors were wearing Caribbean t-shirts with slogans like "Born to sail, forced to work" or "Sail fast, live slow" and making plans for the next few weeks of relaxing cruising in the Caribbean.

Good food and some alcohol had done their work by late afternoon, most adults were dozing in deck chairs and on blankets, keeping a cursory eye on the kids looking for shells on the beach. "Hi, there!" Carla slowly opened her eyes and blinked at Sabine standing in front of her. "Mind if we join you?" The German's two little boys were racing over where the other kids were playing. Carla beckoned next to her and the other women folded out a wooden deck chair she must have brought over from the Super Yacht. "How has your Christmas been," Carla tried to muster some interest. "Oh, we celebrated Christmas yesterday, our Heiligabend, so a quiet day for us three today. Thomas is working, some local deal, he is brokering for a Chinese company to build a new road all along the coast. It will be great for the people here."

Carla had heard about this project from their tour guide, only it was a different story. Chinese companies were building roads everywhere in the Caribbean, they gave the tiny individual countries loans to finance the building works, but were also bringing in their own workers, so no jobs for the locals. The main problem, however, was that the roads crumbled after only a few years while the islands were crippled by the debt burden. "How did he get involved in this?" Carla asked, now with some interest. "He had some links to the Chinese builder when he was still working back in Germany," Sabine answered somewhat vague.

Chapter 17

New Year in Bequia

Port Elizabeth, Bequia's harbour, was a favourite amongst the cruising community. Sailors strolled along the long waterfront with its red ferries, visited the colourful fruit and vege market and enjoyed the many restaurants and cafes and left plenty of EC dollars at the stalls with Caribbean souvenirs.

Hanna and Peter had agreed to pick up a mooring in Bequia, as the holding in front of Princess Margret's beach was known to be poor. Once they had picked a spot Hanna had a look around to see who they knew. "The beautiful Hanseatic is also here, I still haven't looked at that, we should drive over at some stage," Hanna turned to Peter. "First things first," Peter said and pulled the dinghy up. "Let me show you the Pirates of the Caribbean bar with actual photos of Jack Sparrow, I think we deserve a sundowner before the New Year's Eve festivities begin."

Steve on "Dania" like Hanna and Peter just a few hours before, did not trust the holding in front of the popular beach, neither did he completely trust his CQR anchor. "The others are all over there, dad," Leif pointed toward the beach, but Steve shook his head and motored toward the big red mooring buoys near the fuel ship.

Soon after, the family was stocking up with warm bread and croissants at the tiny Port Elizabeth bakery. The town's waterfront was busy and colourful, the promenade had stalls with boat models, vegetables, souvenirs, the Mays just loved the atmosphere. Steve, Carla and the kids hopped on the wooden benches on the tray of a local taxi and zoomed off to the turtle sanctuary. "It is closed," Carla turned from the sign at the door toward her family, dismayed. "But look, mama, there is an old man in there," Leif peeked through the window. The door opened and an elderly local introduced himself as Orton G. King and invited them in.

As they walked from basin to basin Orton explained the plight of the green and hawksbill turtle breeds that cannot survive in sufficient numbers nowadays. He told the children that he takes care of hundreds of turtles of all ages here, feeding and healing them until they are strong enough to survive in the wild. The tiny turtles in the nursery basins were ever so cute while the bigger adults close to the basin's side impressed with their beaks. A true sanctuary for these ancient creatures. Frankie was delighted that there were also several dogs, some tortoises and many tropical birds in cages outside. "I get approached by developers about this piece of real estate all the time but I am not selling," Orton concluded his tour. On their way back in the open taxi the family couldn't stop talking about the baby turtles and their saviour Orton.

Steve and Carla had decided they wanted a family-only dinner on New Year's Eve and join their friends for drinks afterwards. In their finest outfits and in happy spirits they headed ashore to the "L'Auberge Grenadine" restaurant for a lobster dinner. The French-Caribbean place on the water had a great reputation and was praised in all the pilot books for its fresh lobster. "Lucky that he could fit us in for an early sitting," Carla sighed contently, sipping on her first glass of champagne at 6pm while looking across the almost empty restaurant. Frankie and Leif were making bracelets with loom bands, the latest craze in kids' entertainment. It kept them occupied for hours. The caramelized lobster with rum sauce was truly amazing, and the Mays couldn't have been happier with their Caribbean New Year's Eve.

The main festivity for the last day of the year took place on "Chili Cat". A crowd of around twenty adults and the same number of kids from the rally toasted the New Year at midnight and enjoyed the fireworks. As always there was a lot of chatter about other boats and crew, and "Chili Cat" owner Matt, a former Super Yacht captain, contributed the main news of the evening. "Guys, I had a phone call earlier from my mate in St Lucia, the Chinese boat is in, they lifted it straight away and it turns out the rudder stock was cut. Somebody apparently sabotaged it." After a stunned silence everybody started talking. "Who would do such a thing, and why?" "I wonder whether they will find out who it was." "This was a rally, not a race, who would take things so serious?" "Somebody must have dived on 'Saiche" in Las Palmas and had a go at the stock." The family gang speculated for hours. Hanna remembered the yellow dive-generator on the Hanseatic "Elbe" next to the Chinese boat but did not say anything. Diving on boats before a race to take speed-hindering algae off was very common.

Steve had dinghied the tired children back to "Dania" at 2 am after the fireworks and more celebrations, but the adults had partied on ashore. Around 3.30 am Carla had truly enough and was walking to the dinghy dock with Nathan. They had parked their small dinghy there in the afternoon. The bar across from the fruit market was still very busy and Nathan spotted some friends. "Do you mind taking the dinghy by yourself, somebody can drop me over later," he asked. "Sure, not a problem," Carla answered. It would be quite beautiful slowly rowing back to the boat, she thought. Quickly she cast off from the dock, squeezed the dinghy out of the bunch of tenders and started rowing.

The oars were splashing rhythmically in the still water. Carla was gliding toward the three red ferries, tied up together for the New Year's celebration. Where do they normally go to, she didn't even know. She got quite close to one ferry giant when she noticed a dim light shining through the open metal door in the side of the ferry. Actually, it was a torch moving, she saw now. Who was climbing around in the ferry on New Year's morning? Carla knew she should just row past, but her natural curiosity won and she silently manoeuvred the dinghy toward the opening. It would not be easy to get up there through that door from the dinghy, Carla realised, and who knew who was in there, a crazed, doped up local or some villain. So sense prevailed for once and Carla pushed herself off. Louder than expected, the oars made a big splash. A figure appeared in the door way and peered down on her, but it was impossible for her to distinguish any features. She started rowing fast and was soon out of sight, closing in on "Dania". "Better not tell Steve about that," she thought, "He won't let me out of his sight otherwise."

New Year's Day started slow, the children were tired, the adults a bit hung over. Pancakes with maple syrup and bacon seemed the right remedy, Carla had announced, and was busy in the galley. Frankie helped to prepare sugar, lemon and the syrup. Maybe a pyjama and TV day, Carla suggested.

Hanna and Peter had decided to drive across to the Hanseatic "Elbe" a few moorings up as Hanna was curious to see what it looked like down below. "Can we come on board, guys, and have a look at this beauty?" Peter knocked on "Elbe"'s hull, and two heads popped up in the cockpit. Another man seemed asleep in a hammock on the bow. "Sure, ah, hi, Peter, good to see you, come on board" the blonde skipper smiled at them invitingly. Sven was with the tall, ponytailed navigator from "Saiche" whom he introduced as his friend Soren. The two of them beamed at Hanna, they had heard about her. "How about a rum punch you two, Soren and I have already started elevenses," Sven said. There was a half-empty rum bottle, juice and two glasses in the cockpit. Sven signalled Hanna to come down below and look at the interior while he was getting some glasses.

"What a dream fitout," Hanna exclaimed. "So much space and storage. And the woodwork is exceptional!" "We used one tree for the whole inside and made sure the grain ran through from top to bottom in every bulkhead and door." Sven was clearly proud of his boat. They chatted about the boat's features for a while, gossiped about other boats they knew and had another punch. Hanna started to wonder how much the other two had had before they arrived. Sven in particular seemed very animated, even slightly hyper, and talked non-stop.

Peter was curious about "Saiche" and turned toward Soren. "I have heard the boat is back and has been lifted in St Lucia, what have been the findings?" Soren looked uncomfortable but answered: "The titanium rudder stock was too thin for the boat's size. Probably the yard's fault. I only saw the final specs in Las Palmas and complained to the skipper, but he insisted the dimensions would be fine. What was I going to do? However, it also didn't help that somebody worked on the stock with a titanium cutter." "But you need a very special tool to get through titanium," Peter said. "Not many boats will have such a tool on the boat." "We have one," Sven boasted, "I bought it especially in Las Palmas." The German was now slurring his words and clearly had had too much to drink.

A concerned voice came from the hammock at the front. "Sven, Alter, just stop talking. The booze is interfering with your pills." Boat man Mogli swung out of the hammock and wandered to the back. Before his friend even reached the cockpit Sven just stormed down below, a door slammed. "He has been on anti-depressants since his father died," Mogli confided in the shocked trio in the cockpit. "He shouldn't really drink while taking them." Hanna nodded sympathetically. She knew only too well what it was like to lose a father. She had been in therapy for a while after her father's deadly accident while sailing single-handed.

"What did you guys need a titanium cutter for," Peter would not be distracted from the main topic. "You are not going to tell on him, Soren, are you?"Mogli pleaded looking at their friend. "Tell what?" Soren asked with a puzzled look. "You must have guessed by now that Sven has been diving on the Chinese boat in Las Palmas. I can't be completely sure but think he took the cutter down with him. I had been wondering what he bought that thing for, we have no titanium on the boat. That was before we knew you were the navigator but he could hardly tell you what he had done before the start. That's why we kept shadowing you at sea, I believe, to be there if something happened."

A stunned silence was interrupted by Soren's hoarse voice. "So you are telling me that Mr Goody Two Shoes here, famous rescuer of stricken sailors sabotaged my boat, risking our lives? I don't believe it! We have been friends for twenty-five years. Why, on earth?" "I think the yard is in real trouble, he said he needed to win the rally to get all the publicity," Mogli said. The other three had to digest that, nobody spoke. Peter and Hanna decided it was time to leave, they didn't want to witness the likely confrontation between Soren and Sven. So they boarded their dinghy and motored toward "Thea." "That was heavy," Hanna said. "Do we need to tell somebody about it, rally control or the police?" "I am not sure, let's sit on it a bit and think it through," Peter answered.

"After our fun trip to see the turtles, I have decided to write an article about the turtle sanctuary," Carla announced to her family in the afternoon. She also had made no progress on finding out the truth about the Chinese boat's mishap, merely filing a summary with some quotes of crew members to her editor. Carla thought she could publish the turtle article in a local newspaper, the rally newsletter and overseas yachting and nature publications. So on January 2 Carla sat in the open taxi again, heading for an in-depth interview with Orton King.

When she arrived at the turtle sanctuary Carla was surprised to see Thomas Kellermann walk out of the main building. He curtly nodded at her and jumped into the back of a black chauffeur driven car. Carla shook her head, what an aggressive man. After a warm greeting by Orton she asked the old conservationist: "What did that guy want from you just then?" Orton answered: "He wants to buy my land and build a resort, he offered me three million EC dollars. He is representing some American investors he says. But I am not interested in selling. I want to keep looking after my turtles. I don't need all that money I told him. He got quite angry then."

A beach cricket game for the kids later that afternoon attracted most CAR families. After the game the kids swam and played with water toys while the adults were lazing on the beach. Steve was asleep on his towel, Carla next to him immersed in the latest Inspector Dupin crime novel. A shadow fell over her book and Carla squinted into the sun. Thomas Kellerman stared down at her clearly looking for confrontation: "Sabine just told me you are a journalist. I didn't know that. I would advise strongly for you to stay out of my affairs." His voice was staccato, aggressive, and maybe a bit nervous. Carla didn't reply and just stared back, she had dealt with bullies like him before. What was he so wound up about, she wondered? Should she start digging or just leave it be? She didn't need any stress, this was after all a holiday from all that.

The rally family fleet left Bequia a few days into the New Year to head for the Tobago Cays. As the boats motored out, many noticed a whole headland full of building ruins of what must have been planned as a large resort right next to Princess Margret Beach. Just a bit further a small freighter sat firmly on the rocks. A different world.

Chapter 18

Tobago Cays

"Look, there is the rock that Jack Sparrow sailed past in the opening scene of the first movie," Leif was an expert on the Pirates of the Caribbean movies. He was peeking through the boat's binoculars. "We are not going there, mate, it is too dangerous," his father said firmly. Most boats took a wide berth around St Vincent, an island that had a reputation for violence, boat robberies and even murder. Not that long ago a boat was entered and a German sailor killed in front of his family. "Dania"'s crew had felt completely safe in the Caribbean so far, not alone because former Royal Marine Nathan was sleeping on deck. But one needn't tempt fate. "There is a few boats with CAR flags in the bay, brave people, isn't that the new Hanse of that Polish guy that Hanna had trouble with?" Steve pointed at a boat close to the shore. Carla took the binoculars and had a closer look. "Yes, that is "Gdynia", I wonder why he would risk going there."

"Dania" was soon nosing through the shallow passage between Petit Rameau and Petit Bateau, Steve keeping a close eye on the echo sounder for depth, adjusting his course frequently. The water was a bright turquois and looked really shallow in places. "Let's not anchor inside the outer reef, it's too windy," Steve pointed toward the horse shoe reef where two brave catamarans were pitching heavily on their anchor. "Just pick up one of those three moorings, there behind Baradol's sand spit," he instructed Nathan. An hour after the Grand Central Station atmosphere of their arrival, with boats leaving everywhere, soon there were only about ten boats left. It was the end of New Year holiday and the charter boats had to get back to their base.

The Tobago Cays is a special place, considered the highlight of any Windward Island cruise. Snorkelling in the turtle sanctuary is a fantastic wild life experience especially for children. The "Dania" family was soon in the water snorkelling with the green turtles near Baradol. "The turtles are so cute, but I am cold now. Let's go to the beach," Frankie commanded. The sanctuary was fenced off with a net, but dinghies could carefully motor through to the beach. Nathan helped Frankie and Leif build a sandcastle on Baradol's sand spit in clear view of the island that Jack Sparrow was marooned on.

In the afternoon the wind had eased, and the "Dania" crew went on a little excursion with the rubber duckie. "There, that is that big boat that Leon and Markus are on," Leif expertly pointed. "Looks like it is blocking the channel." Leif was right, the Super yacht the Germans had chartered was anchored right in the narrow approach, making it difficult for other boats to get past. "Let's pay them a visit," Steve suggested. Carla frowned but nodded her consent. "I would love to see what it is like inside, it looks like it could have been built in Turkey, I am sure the craftsmanship is excellent," Steve said. Carla was not completely sure they were welcome but nevertheless knocked on the hull near the bathing ladder. Sabine Kellermann peeked over the side and smiled. "Oh, it's you, come on board, Markus and Leon will be glad to have some company." The kids scrambled up the ladder followed by their parents and disappeared straight into the cabin, yelling for the little boys.

"Let me show you around, the boat is gorgeous," Sabine said, adding: "Thomas is not here, he took the RIB somewhere." Sabine led them along the spacious deck area into the yacht. It had a real dining room and comfortable saloon with sofas, and down some steps they noticed lots of shiny doors into cabins. "You got to see this," Sabine opened the door to the master cabin. Carla couldn't believe her eyes: "A free standing bath tub! What utter luxury, we don't even have a proper shower." While Sabine was pointing out the clever lighting system to Steve, Carla went over to the mahogany desk and admired its inlay in the shape of a schooner. She pushed a pile of paper to the side to better see the wood work when an angry voice boomed: “What on earth are you doing with my papers?” Carla spun around, facing an irate Thomas Kellermann. “I was just admiring the fantastic intarsia in the wood, I didn’t look at your papers, don’t worry,” she smiled. “We were just going to have a drink, are you joining us, darling,” Sabine Kellermann tried to diffuse the tension. “No, I had forgotten these papers, I am off again, see you at dinner.” With that he turned and left. The three others finished their guided tour in the kids play room, where the four children were happily watching a movie. Steve soon got chatting to the Australian Super Yacht skipper and was invited to an inspection of the engine room while the women were drinking iced tea in some deck chairs at the back. “How civilized is this boat, much less work than sailing our tub, I am envious,” Carla smiled at Sabine.

At happy hour time Carla was reading a book in the cockpit when from a close-by French boat a shrill voice shouted across: “Your boat is moving, vite, vite, do something!” Carla lifted her head off the bean bag, assessed the situation and in a calm tone replied: ”You are drifting toward us, Madam, we are on a mooring. Your anchor must be dragging.” Carla settled back into her bean bag, smiling. Life was good! She was particularly looking forward to their lobster dinner ashore on Petit Bateau at the shack that night. “Was that the best lobster ever?” Steve asked his daughter, a little woman with expensive tastes. “Dad, that was amazing, thanks!” Frankie beamed at him. The platter with big lobsters accompanied by the local fried bananas had been out of this world.

Snorkelling over the outer reef the next morning, Carla was glad they had left the kids on the boat with Nathan. Due to the strengthening wind there was a considerable chop, and they got really wet just motoring over to the reef in the dinghy. Under water life was peaceful, though, and Carla was soon gliding over the colourful coral with different tropical fish and the odd turtle. Steve was looking at a small wreck to her left while Carla was trying to take some photos of a grazing green turtle. The water creatures fascinated her, and the photos would complement her article well. Pausing again, Carla lifted her underwater camera to capture a hawksbill turtle this time. Maybe I can get a bit closer, she thought. The turtle turned her head and started swimming. Carla followed closely.

The new camera worked great, Carla took shot after shot of the grazing turtle moving away from the wreck and Steve. What was that movement? She felt something cold, a stream of water gushing along her right hand side. She looked down at her body. What was this, a big fish, was there sharks here? Carla started to panic, moved her face with the snorkel mask to the left and right, she was never completely comfortable under water. Looking forward she saw a black menacing stick disappear into the murk, a spear from a spear gun! It had whooshed closely past her hip. She looked back to see who had shot the gun but could not detect anybody. Steve was still poking around the wreck and had apparently not noticed anything. Carla swam toward her husband as fast as she could, waving her arms, signalling him that she was swimming back to the dinghy. "It would have been an accident for sure," Steve tried to calm her down when they had both climbed back into the dinghy and Carla had told him what had happened. "You are not allowed to spear-gun here, who would do such a thing in a tourist area. What if it was not an accident but an attack because I have asked too many uncomfortable questions somewhere?" Carla wasn't convinced.

Meanwhile on the super yacht Sabine Kellermann was confronting her husband. "Do me a favour and put that dangerous thing away. The boys might hurt themselves on it. And why do you have to zoom off again to a meeting, leaving us. The point of this trip was you spending more time with the boys." "Maybe for you that was the point, but not for me. I will be back tomorrow," her husband coolly answered, and turned to the waiting rib that was driving him at mach speed across to Grenada. He zipped up his spray jacket, knowing it would be a long, bumpy ride. But he had to get there for tomorrow morning, it was vital he participated in the meeting. This deal would get him out of the financial strap he got himself into.

“I will be back here tomorrow at noon,” Thomas Kellermann instructed the rib driver when he stepped onto the quay in Sauteurs on the northern tip of Grenada. He had booked a room above a pub for the night and after he had checked in made his way across to a restaurant. He needed an early night to have his wits together for tomorrow’s meeting.

Chapter 19

St Vincent Pirates

The big bay behind the reef in Union Island was full of yachts when "Dania" arrived in the late afternoon, but the Australian family found a sizable mooring, and Steve soon made his way to the administration building near the airport. Clearing into the little country St Vincent and the Grenadines was also possible in Union Island, and many crews chose a short pit stop there to avoid going to St Vincent. The May kids Leif and Frankie thought the light planes landing over their heads were fantastic, and Carla pointed out the kite surfers zooming inside the half-moon shaped outer reef.

Pavel had waved Elsbeth's concern away. "All that hype about St Vincent being dangerous, all rubbish, we are going to show the punters where Jack Sparrow landed!" Wallilabou Bay had been used to film the first Pirates of the Caribbean movie, and the bunch of Americans that had joined "Gdynia" after Christmas was keen to visit the movie set.

"Gdynia" had arrived late in the bay and Pavel had carefully chosen an anchor spot close to the shore. Everybody was looking forward to the sightseeing day ahead. Dinner and after dinner drinks had finished at 11pm and the crew went to bed. As so often when he had guests on board, Pavel had suggested for him and Elsbeth to sleep in the cockpit. Just after 1am Elsbeth woke up. There was a scraping noise at the stern, a faint squeak, she pushed herself onto her elbows and to her horror saw three men silently climbing up the swim ladder. Frantically, Elsbeth started to shake Pavel on the other side of the cockpit. He jumped up at once. "Hey, man, stay where you are and give us your valuables," a local addressed Pavel and waved a shotgun at him. "You there, unfasten the dinghy," he then motioned towards Elsbeth. "We have little money, we are just tourists," Pavel tried without success. "Give me the fucking money," the rasta-haired guy with typical Caribbean beanie shouted now. The other two were climbing into the cabin, harassing the charter guests.

Elsbeth had climbed into the dinghy but couldn't unfasten it. "I don't have the key, I cannot get the lock open," she told the gang leader that seemed more and more impatient. "Give her the key, man, and go and get the money!" Pavel did not move but one of the American guests climbed up the companionway ladder to hand out some money and credit cards. The chief pirate kicked the American into the ribcage, the guest fell heavily back into the cabin. Another pirate waved a machete around the poor guy's face and collected the money and cards. "The dinghy, man, what are you waiting for?" Elsbeth looked at Pavel who seemed frozen to his spot in the cockpit and did not move. "Pavel, give him the key, please!" Elsbeth tried to reason with her boyfriend, to no avail. The gang leader now with a bundle of cash and some cards in his hand again turned toward Pavel, just lifted his shotgun and shot him at point blank.

Elsbeth felt like being in a movie, a bad one. In slow motion Pavel dropped onto the cockpit floor, blood pouring out of his chest. The pirates left hastily now, climbing into a little speed boat. Elsbeth woke up from her stupor, jumped down the stairs and grabbed the flare gun. She shot a red signal into the sky and in the glow could see that the little pirate boat was heading toward the village. Then she grabbed the handheld VHF and started calling "Mayday. Mayday, Mayday."

It took an endless 15 minutes before an English doctor from a neighbouring boat came to help Pavel. Elsbeth had tried to stem the blood flow with a tea towel, but there was a lot of blood, and Pavel was extremely pale by now. "He needs to get to a hospital at once, but I don't think they have helicopters here, let's take him ashore in the dinghy," the English doctor sighed after bandaging Pavel's chest. Getting the lifeless skipper into the RIB needed four of the crew, Elsbeth went along with boat papers and passports, holding Pavel's hand. The only hospital was in the capital Kingstown, and Elsbeth felt the journey in the ambulance took forever. Finally arrived, things started moving fast, a stretcher was rolled out and at great speed Pavel was wheeled into an operating theatre. Elsbeth collapsed onto a wooden bench outside the theatre, crying. The waiting began.

On this beautiful Caribbean morning not far from St Vincent but worlds away, Carla was on a mission to find Union Island's pharmacy. The kids had nits! When the first radio messages about head lice had circulated amongst the CAR parents Carla could not believe it. But inspecting the children's hair it was soon confirmed, they were crawling with them. Not only that, maybe because Carla had admitted to the problem early on via the radio, other parents seemed to be of the impression their kids had caught the nits from Leif and Frankie, which was just not true. Whatever, Carla needed a fine comb and some anti-nit shampoo. Not an easy task as it turned out, the local children didn't seem to get them. Carla found a comb and decided to just use conditioner on the children's hair. That would also do the trick. What a pain! Carla's scalp was itching just thinking about nits.

After trapsing around the village for hours in the heat and then a big lunch everybody was tired. Dad had shouted them all burgers on the terrace of a small restaurant, a good ending to a busy day. Only next morning when checking his emails Nathan noticed a message from his bank at home in the UK. They had blocked his credit card after some suspicious transactions in Union Island, the message said. "It must have been swiped at the ATM last night when I got some money," Nathan sighed.

Back on "Dania" the VHF crackled into life and Steve answered the voice calling his boat's name. Carla joined him on the chart table seat and they were stunned to hear from Hanna that the Polish skipper Pavel had been shot on St Vincent. "He is alive, barely," Hanna said. "Elsbeth is beside herself, she has asked us to help move the boat to Union, so Pete and I are flying over tomorrow. The charter guests have left straight away, understandably." Steve promised to keep an eye on "Thea", moored a bit to the left of them, and they finished the call. What a nightmare!

Chapter 20

Grenada

"Ok, kids, here is what you need to know before we do the bus trip around the island. Yes, school is officially over, but it doesn't hurt to have a bit of background before we go." Steve had a travel guide in his hand and was reading out facts about the spice island Grenada to his family at breakfast. At 10am a guide would collect them in a minivan and drive them around the island.

The "Dania" crew had arrived in the capital St George the day before, enjoying a blistering reach down the Grenada coast. "I didn't tell you about the areas of volcanic activity we might have crossed, I guessed we would see the bubbles," Carla had confessed to Steve when they motored into the wide harbour entrance. For cost reasons they had decided against mooring in the brand new Port Louis marina but instead had squeezed into a berth next to the petrol station in the yacht club opposite. The clubhouse with its wraparound veranda and chunky chairs had a true colonial feeling and food was cheap here, but the showers were incredibly mosquito infested, and the Australian family decided to move to the chic marina the next morning. Two other CAR families were there already, and more were expected.

British entrepreneur Peter de Savary had taken a close look at Grenada after hurricane Ivan hit the island. He was hoping to convert the swampy lagoon into a St Tropez style glitzy resort with hotels, villas and the marina. Savary had come a long way, the Port Louis marina was nicely filled and the CAR families bought t-shirts and souvenirs for home at the upmarket little shops. "Dania" was moored at the furthest dock to the East, quite a walk ashore.

"The island is 18 km wide and 34 km long and around 110,000 people live here. Christopher Columbus discovered Grenada in 1498.

The island was already inhabited by the Carib Indians, who had migrated from the South American mainland, killing or enslaving the peaceful Arawaks who were living on the island," Steve was reading. "In 1877 Grenada became a British Crown Colony, and in 1967 it became an associate state within the British Commonwealth before gaining independence in 1974. In 1979, an attempt was made to set up a socialist/communist state in Grenada. Four years later, at the request of the Governor General, the United States, Jamaica, and the Eastern Caribbean States intervened militarily. Launching their now famous "rescue mission," the allied forces restored order, and in December of 1984 a general election re-established democratic government."

Steve put the travel guide into his backpack. The kids by now had switched off and were playing with Lego, but Carla was glad to refresh her memory of what had happened on the island. Carla didn't remember much about Grenada's distant past but had reported on the island's recent disaster as a journalist. Hurricane Ivan in September 2004 put a stop to the firm belief that Grenada was hurricane safe. The destruction had been of epic proportions. Barely a building stood whole, barely a house had a roof. Ninety percent of the buildings on the island had been damaged, thirty percent of which needed complete rebuilding. Carla remembered that the main German yacht insurer had a damage inspector live on the island for a year, as most yachts stored here for the hurricane season had been blown over, tangles of broken hulls and rigs, boats sunken or heavily damaged. In 2005 another hurricane struck, Emily, laying devastation to the island's north and adding to its misery.

The family climbed into the blue van with its smiling driver who introduced himself as Willie. He drove them through the lush, green landscape with its colourful villages, busy rum stalls along the road, everything a bit run down. The spice trade, mainly nutmeg but also cinnamon, ginger, allspice and many more had traditionally been the mainstay of Grenada's economy, but nowadays tourism was the big earner. The building of the new cruise ship terminal in St George had made a huge difference. However, the hurricanes had had a crippling effect on the economy.

"Only 15 percent of private homes had been insured, and after the disaster suicide rates soared on the island, everybody had lost hope," their guide Willie sighed. "Now we are a really young island, as so many middle aged people are dead. But because there was not much left after the hurricane people built on their strong sense of family, they helped each other and in the end made this a better community." Quite clearly Grenada had only slowly managed to recover from the catastrophe.

Willi knew that Chinese companies were financing and delivering some of the building works on the island as on so many other Caribbean islands. But there were also some American investors, he said. Who benefitted most was to be seen. "The new High School in St George where my son goes already has cracks in the walls, these building are not made to last."

In Sauteurs Willie stopped the car in front of a restaurant and although it was only 12 o' clock chirpily announced: "Lunchtime!" Steve wondered whether the restaurant owner was a friend of Willie's, but the kids didn't have to be asked twice and raced through the beady entrance curtain. Only two of the ten tables inside were occupied, and to Carla's dismay she spotted Thomas Kellermann with his back to them in deep conversation with two Chinese and a local man, sitting at a table near the kitchen door. Fortunately he hadn't noticed them, and the family took a table at the big window to be able to observe the street life.

Thomas Kellermann's meeting wasn't going to plan at all. Beads of sweat had formed on his forehead while he tried to keep the all-important negotiations on track. "The quality of the interior fitout is just sub-standard, we will not accept it," the local man with short cropped hair said firmly. "What exactly do you mean by substandard, Mr Conroy?" the tone of one of the Chinese men was openly hostile. "The project is late, the build quality unacceptable, so we will withhold the last tranche of the overall payment," the other man remained unfazed. "The second, older Chinese man got agitated: "We have a contract, you must pay, otherwise we sue!"" Now, now, gentlemen,"Kellermann interrupted. "Accusations are not getting us any further here. Why don't we work out a precise work schedule toward the soft opening of the resort. I am sure it can't be that much that remains to be done. Mr Conroy, just tell me your and the Dwyer family's concerns and our very competent builder here, Mr Bao, will address the issues."

"What was the best bit of our trip, children?" Steve asked the usual family question at the end of their tour. "I liked the rum distillery best, dad," Leif answered. "Really?" Steve looked surprised. "No, dad, just kidding, the chocolate factory! I thought you would like the rum distillery but you made a real face tasting the rum." "I thought it was fascinating to see how they make the rum, those huge basins with that grey, dirty looking liquid in them, and those mountains of sugar cane leaves, amazing. The finished product was a bit rough for me, though. How about the chocolate?" "Same, dad, a bit rough, I prefer milk chocolate to dark anyway." Leif grinned.

"Before we get back to the harbour I will show you something special," guide Willie turned off the main road toward the coast. "Hold on everybody," he said and hit the accelerator while the kids started to squeal. The van was flying, going faster and faster, down the runway of what had been Grenada's Pearls Airport in the north part of the island, now derelict. The unfinished new International Airport in the southwest had been the jump off point for the invasion by American troops in October 1983, it was now fully functional. Willie was giving it heaps, the van was almost taking off. They were zooming at breakneck speed, past an overgrown passenger plane toward the water. Everybody squealed. Finally Willie braked and the car came to a shuddering standstill. "That was such fun, Willie," Leif shouted with shining eyes. The adults also grinned from ear to ear, everybody had loved that grand finale to their trip.

Chapter 21

Confessions

"Look, there is "Thea", and Hanna is here," Frankie's sharp eyes had spotted the Swan on the outside jetty. After a big hello and nicely settled in the Swan's back cockpit, Hanna told them what she had found on her trip to St Vincent. Peter had stayed on "Thea" after all, one of his projects had gone off the rails, and he needed to be on the phone and computer for a few days.

"Travelling to Wallilabou Bay from the airport was no problem, I just took a taxi" she started. "I phoned Elsbeth and she collected me in the dinghy. But I have never seen her so shaken, she was white as a sheet. Sounds like Pavel is very badly injured, the shot hit his lung and part of the stomach, but he will pull through. But that was not all the bad news!"

Elsbeth had told Hanna that Pavel apparently had well advanced plans to supplement his charter income with running drugs out of Columbia, and had taken a first shipment on board already. "I don't know when he got the packets," Elsbeth had cried. "It must have been one night somewhere on the way down, possibly a courier in a little boat delivering it. I certainly didn't notice anything. But after everybody had left and Pavel was settled in hospital I gave the boat a thorough clean, also to take my mind off things, and I found kilos of cocaine under the front floorboards. He admitted to it when I confronted him after he regained consciousness. Apparently that tosser Urs was the middle man who knew the producers in Columbia. He came on our boat as a cover. What am I going to do with that stuff, Hanna?"

Hanna had been shocked. This was serious. "Well, we can't sail around with kilos of drugs, if somebody inspects the boat we end up in jail. We have to get rid of them straight away, tonight." So the girls got through a long, tense evening, sitting and dozing in "Gdynia's" cockpit until 2am when they lifted anchor and slowly motored to sea. Two miles offshore they got the drug parcels on deck, cut them open with scissors and let the white powder sink into the ocean. Hanna then carefully hosed the deck with the deck shower and very reluctantly sank the plastic bags with a stone to the ocean floor. Bad for the environment but utterly necessary. Completely drained by the tension and anxiety they dropped anchor again around 4.30 am and fell into their bunks, Hanna told her friends. "What an absolute nightmare! Where are "Gdynia" and Elsbeth now?" "We sailed across the next day. I left her at Union Island, collected Peter and "Thea" and we came here. Peter has met a mate and is having a beer on some boat now. I will have a lie down now, see you a bit later."

"Kids, stop fighting, I couldn't even hear what Hanna was saying! Darling, how about getting the Opti off the deck to let them have a sail around the harbour?" The Optimist dinghy had been secured to the deck during the Atlantic crossing and was salt crusted. "Leif, you take the hose, Frankie, you the sponge," their father commanded. An hour went by before the little boat was finally afloat with the two children now fighting over the helm. Steve and Carla hopped in the rubber duckie to coach them along.

"The further south we get, the better the rum punches are," Carla gave a content little sigh, sipping on her second glass a few hours later. The family had dinner with Peter and Hanna at the nice pizza place next to the pool. The kids were yelling and splashing in the water, the adults supervising from their table while waiting for the wheel-sized pizzas to arrive. Hanna seemed a bit recovered from the excitement of the last few days. "And here is our pretentious friend again, god, we can't escape him," Carla remarked, pointing at the wooden super yacht the Kellermanns had chartered. It had taken a big boat berth outside the pool area. Soon they watched the whole family disembark and walk off toward the shops.

"Cheers, so what's new in the CAR world apart from the St Vincent drama?" Steve clicked his glass on Peter's. "Well, there is no further news about the Poldi story, he has disappeared without a trace, which I guess is good. Hans and Susie are still in St Lucia with their family," Peter was happy to report. The four friends exchanged some more news about other crews.

Peter looked at Hanna and hesitated: "Steve, Carla, I need your advice on something Hanna and I heard yesterday, it is confidential information and I am not quite sure what to do about it." He felt guilty about letting out the secret behind "Saiche"'s accident, but the men on "Elbe" must have been aware that he would talk to somebody, even the police. "More by coincidence we got told how the rudder on "Saiche" failed, and I am not sure whether to pass on the information to the officials," Pete began. "It looks like another boat owner cut the rudder stock before the start to gain an advantage. He had desperate reasons for that, but still put the Chinese boat's crew in danger. Would you report that to rally control?"

"Sabotage, naturally you have to report that," Steve was outraged. "It was Sven from "Elbe", wasn't it, it makes sense, he didn't want the competition. He needed to make his boat a success," Carla guessed. Surprised, Peter just nodded. This was a fantastic story, but Carla knew she wouldn't write it. "You know, I feel sorry for the guy," she said. "His family firm with so much tradition, his father now dead, money worries." Steve shook his head: "Just because he saved the others in the end does not mean he mustn't owe up to what he did." Peter was torn, no closer to knowing whether to pass on the information to rally control or not. "I think you should ask Sven Martens to admit what he has done to rally control and ask them to try to limit the negative publicity," Hanna suggested. "Not sure that will work, this will be big news!" Carla sighed.

Chapter 22

Russian Cargo

Carla needed to clear her head from all the recent drama, although she was sure their little family was only on the sidelines and safe. Still, she felt her Caribbean dream tainted by violence and deceit, she needed to distract herself. Camera on her shoulder she hailed a taxi at the marina entrance and told the driver to get her to the old Pearls Airport in the Northeast. She wanted to take some photos for a cruising story. The kids were in the pool again with some other kids, supervised by their kind parents, and Steve was discussing Grenada boat yards with a local boatman.

The old Russian cargo plane with the runway and turquoise ocean in the background made for great photos, Carla was happily snapping away, oblivious of her surroundings. She pushed closer through the high grass and pulled away some weeds from the plane door. The cockpit looked surprisingly well preserved. When she was just about to climb into the hold somebody touched her shoulder. Carla jumped, but quickly composed herself when she saw who it was. "We seem to bump into each other all the time," Carla tried an innocent smile. "Not you again," the tall man answered much less friendly. "You just can't keep your nose out of other people's affairs. I saw you at the restaurant up north. Why are you here?" He came menacingly close. "Just taking a few scenic shots," she tried to pacify him. "A journalist just taking a few harmless shots, well, well,"Kellermann looked at her, calculating. "You have nothing to hide, have you Thomas," Carla snapped back. "How about that Chinese dude I saw you with in that restaurant, up to some dirty business?"

A look of pure hatred shot across Kellermann's face and he surprised Carla by pushing her backwards through the open plane door and closing it with a bang. Ouch, that hurt. Carla had fallen heavily on her backside. Disoriented, in semi-darkness Carla looked for the unlocking mechanism. But the Russian door was unlike a modern plane door, it was old fashioned, just a handle, that Kellermann must have jammed something under so she couldn't open it. Nor did the cockpit door budge. Carla started to bang on the plane's metal hull with a stick, it made a huge noise. "Thomas, don't be ridiculous, let me out! Help, help, anybody, I am stuck in here!" she shouted. After ten minutes her arms grew tired and she sat on the planes floor, occasionally hitting the wall next to her with the stick.

Eventually she got up and looked at other options. She pulled the door to the cockpit toward her, this time really hard. It flung open with a bang and Carla entered the derelict cockpit that was overgrown with weeds and grass. The window had smashed years ago and Carla started to fight her way through the vegetation toward the opening. "Can I help you," a very plush British voice sounded from outside. "Yes, please, can you open the door for me," Carla asked and returned into the hold. The sun was shining through the now open doorway and Carla felt utterly relieved.

"Sorry, I didn't introduce myself. I am Charles Dwyer," a blonde man in his mid-thirties smiled at her as if they had just met at the Ascot races. "Are you related to the Dwyer hotel family," Carla couldn't stop herself from asking. "Yes, my brother Henry runs the family firm, but I am also working there as a director." "Thanks for saving me, some idiot locked me in and I was just trying to climb through the window," she shook his outstretched hand. "How utterly rude, did you know the man?" Carla's saviour frowned. He must have gone to an elite school in England, Carla silently admired Charles Dwyer's accent. "Yes, he is a fellow sailor I have met before, for some reason he doesn't like my face."

Charles Dwyer steered Carla to his Morgan sports car, what else, and drove her to a plantation style mansion to wash her hands and face. "Let's have some tea and scones after that fright," Charles suggested and called a house maid. Carla really enjoyed herself on the large veranda, she felt a bit like in "Gone with the Wind". Charles was easy to talk to, and yes, he had gone to Eton and Cambridge, but had returned to Grenada after finishing his English degree to work in the family hotel business. "We are currently building a new resort down south," Charles explained. "I was just checking whether this runway could be upgraded for private jets. The waiting times at the new airport can be horrendous and some of our guests might decide to come in their own plane." After an interesting hour of conversation Charles organised a car to get Carla back to the marina.

"You wouldn't believe what happened to me," Carla exclaimed when she jumped down the companionway steps that were firmly back in place. Steve sat at the chart table pouring over some boat manual. Carla squeezed next to him, planted a kiss on his cheek and started telling him about her afternoon adventure. "This is outrageous, I feel like punching the guy, but maybe you are right, we need to keep an eye on him and try to stay out of his way, he seems ruthless, I don't want you hurt," Steve concluded their conversation.

After dinner with the kids tucked into their bunks Carla sat down and did some serious research, she was curious now. What was Thomas Kellermann up to? The good internet at the marina made things so much easier. She soon struck gold with a recent press release:

"The $4 billion USD project is called the Hog Island Resort, which officially launched in China.
The project plans to develop the Mt Hartman peninsula and Hog Island in Grenada; it would include high-end resorts, a wellness centre and other recreational and entertainment features, according to a statement from the Grenadian government. It is being developed by a Chinese company called Freedom Group, spearheaded by Grenada's commercial attache at its Beijing embassy, Frederic Wong. Agent for the deal is lawyer Thomas Kellermann from Hamburg, Germany. The project would be the latest major Chinese tourism project in the Caribbean, following Nassau's Baha Mar and a recently-launched project in Antigua and Barbuda."

Digging deeper, Carla found out lots more. Hog Island did belong to her new friend Charles' family, the Dwyers, British luxury hoteliers with a long tradition. They had wanted to develop the island for ages but lacked big scale funds. The planned luxury resort with four hotels, its own private island, wellness center, casino and golf course almost became a victim of the 2008 Great Financial Crisis when investors started pulling out. Then China stepped in. Thanks to a $2.4 billion loan from China's export-import bank, an injection of development cash and 4,000 Chinese workers the project was salvaged.

The Chinese had invested at least $8.2 billion so far in the Caribbean and Central America in the last decade, Carla learned. They were still ploughing billions into the Caribbean market. Projects like the Baha Mar in the Bahamas, a resort in Antigua and Barbuda, a biopesticide plant in Cuba and a new $50 billion canal in Nicaragua to rival the Panama Canal were all ambitious projects.

The resort in Grenada would allegedly create 5,000 jobs and make a huge contribution to GDP, the government was hoping, possibly more than 10 percent. But more so, it would help to reduce the horrendous debt load of its cash-strapped government. Grenada's creditors restructured $262 million in global debt in 2015. Caribbean countries are some of the most indebted countries in the world.

Now disputes between the builder, China Building and the Dwyer Family had evolved into a public sparring match about the again and again delayed opening. "It has become clear that our contractor has not completed the work with an attention to detail consistent with our standards of excellence," a Dwyer press release said. Clearly the family with a reputation for the utmost quality in their hotels was not happy to push back the soft opening of the Hog Island resort, and now even the real opening was being pushed back. In a response the Chinese company refuted criticism as "wholly inappropriate" but would have to fix this flagship project.

So that explained Thomas Kellermann appearing everywhere in the islands, Carla decided. He likely was the middle man for Chinese developers in various projects that promised huge financial gain. And the biggest project apparently was going off the rails. Kellermann clearly didn't want a journalist snooping around. Well, they would be leaving Grenada to fly home in a few days, she just had to stay out of his way until then. With a decisive bang Carla shut her laptop and joined Steve in the cockpit.

An ice cream run was necessary in the afternoon and the May family dinghied ashore. They ended up at the beach bar at Princess Margret Beach with a whole lot of other CAR families. The children built sand castles and splashed around while the adults were sipping a happy hour punch. Sabine Kellermann was in the crowd but Carla kept a distance to her, not really wanting to even get into a conversation with her.

But she needn't worried, the conflict came to her. Thomas Kellermann walked by, very close to Carla's towel, kicking sand onto it and smirking at her. "Had a good time flying the other day," he said. Carla felt anger boil up and hissed at him in German: "You utter pratt, I could have been in there for hours, completely unacceptable behaviour. What is your problem, asshole, am I getting too close to some of your little secrets?" Kellermann's smile froze, he was going to say something but saw Steve walking up, and so just walked off in the other direction. Steve looked questioningly at Carla, but she gave him a reassuring wave and he returned to the group of men under an umbrella.

"What was that about," Hanna who was lying next to Carla, asked her friend, astounded. She hadn't understood the German exchange but clearly got the vibe. "The man is an idiot, we have had a few run-ins, he is worried I am onto his dubious businesses," Carla answered.

Chapter 23

Hog Island

Hog Island Bay was the last hurrah for the CAR family fleet. Some boats were now sailing north to eventually finish the Atlantic loop with another crossing to Europe. Others were heading toward the Panama Canal via the Dutch Antilles, St Blas Islands and Columbia, while a small minority put their boats up in a marina here to return for some more Caribbean sailing next season. The boat yards and marinas on the south coast of Grenada had a good reputation. "Dania"'s insurer had recommended Grenada Marine, so that's where the Australian family was heading in two days.

"Frankie, darling, are you sure you can swim that far? If you run out of steam just wave and I will come and tow you." Carla in her red swimsuit stood at "Dania's" rail watching anxiously as her seven-year old daughter jumped from the bow with a squeal. Once resurfaced she swam toward "Chilicat" where her friend Luciana was impatiently waiting for her for a playdate. Luciana's dad had just relayed that message. Steve and Leif had left in the dinghy, so Frankie had resolutely declared she would swim to her friend, no problem. It was a fair distance to swim, but all the CAR kids swam well by now, and Carla let her have a go. The children had come such a long way from cautious city dwellers to independent spirits, completely comfortable in nature. Carla looked around the bay, 12 CAR family boats were anchored here, what a blast. "I will miss everybody once we part ways," she thought. She spotted one family having lunch in the cockpit, on another boat the usual drinks gathering was in full swing. Two brave dads were towing five boys on a paddle board, another dinghy was gathering children for a snorkelling expedition. This was living the dream.

Carla sighed with relief once she saw Frankie climb up the ladder of the big catamaran and disappear into the cabin. "I might have to swim over to collect her later," she decided and went down below to do some writing.

Her turtle article was almost finished and Carla was very pleased with it. Hopefully it would rally support for the animal sanctuary and deter greedy developers. At the end she put down Orton King's donation website. The turtle king deserved all the support he could get.

After lunch and a nap Steve suggested a little family trip to check out the newly built resort on Hog Island. They jumped into the dinghy and with their two horse power outboard chugged toward the left hand side of the bay where they could see the new buildings.

"They have built a proper dinghy dock, let's tie up there," Steve was pleased. Everybody jumped out and strolled toward what at some stage would be the promenade, but still was covered in sand and gravel now. They admired the subtle architecture of loosely connected pavilions clad in wood and surrounded by greenery, the buildings blending into the Caribbean jungle. This was so unlike the sister project Baha Mar in the Bahamas. Carla had shown Steve photos of the pompous resort that could equally have been built in superlative crazy Dubai with its turrets and lagoon. "This looks environmentally friendly, in sync with its surroundings, I think it will be great!" Carla exclaimed.

"I certainly hope so," a smiling Charles Dwyer had appeared out of nowhere. "And this must be your family, my dear Carla." Steve looked surprised when the suave businessman kissed his blushing wife on both cheeks. After proper introductions were made, Charles offered the Australian family a guided tour of the resort. "The resort aims at high-netting individuals who value their privacy above all. All accommodation is free standing, villas and houses. We are trying to lure the Mick Jaggers and Price Williams away from Mustique, but will also cater to wealthy families with children. We did a lot of market research and think we have the concept right." "Frankie, Leif, be careful on that bridge!" Carla called after her children running ahead. Charles led the Australian family across a long wooden swinging bridge. They strolled between more pavilions toward the central square. "Here everything, and everybody will come together, imitating an Italian plaza. We have cafes, bars, several restaurants. There will be boutiques, book shops, it will be a place where people like to spend their lunchtime or evening." Charles was very enthusiastic about his family's flagship development.

"This is very impressive, I wish we were high-net individuals." Steve said. "It looks fairly finished, when are you opening?" Charles smiled and answered: "Naturally you will get the family and friends discount when booking, I will get your details before you leave. But an opening is not on the cards for a while, unfortunately, we are having problems with the builder." Now at the end of their tour, the little group was approaching the dinghy dock again. To Carla and Steve's surprise, a smiling Thomas Kellermann stepped forward and greeted Charles Dwyer reverently: "Charles, how nice to see you. Have you got a moment for me?" Charles answered tersely: "Not now, mein Herr, not the time."

The German looked stunned, turned on his heel and disappeared toward the building site. Charles, seeing his guests puzzled expressions, explained: "He is the agent for the Chinese, and not in the good books with me at the moment. He is avoiding all discussions about regress and completion but constantly pushes me to pay the Chinese builder more money, which I will not do. He is quite an annoying character." "Tell me about it," Carla said. "He was the one locking me into the plane, he considers my journalistic background a danger.

Charles added firmly: "My family wants this resort finished to the highest standard in line with our overall concept and tradition. We will not accept the sub-standard quality that we are seeing right now with this builder. We also don't want to get burned like the people in the Bahamas. Last June, our sister resort Baha Mar filed for bankruptcy blaming the Chinese contractor, also our contractor, for the delays that caused the grand opening of the resort to be postponed several times. The Chinese company has said it wasn't responsible for the delays and attributed them to mismanagement by the developer. Work has stopped on that site for over a year now. We are trying to handle things differently here. We are going to use a contractor from the UK and finish the building within six weeks. The Chinese don't like that one bit."

"What a mess, so what is happening at Baha Mar now?" Steve asked with interest. He was working as a civil engineer for a construction company back in Australia. "Several groups have been talking to the China Export-Import Bank, which financed $2.45 billion of the resort, in hopes of taking over and completing the project. But the resort's original developer also wants a crack at completing the resort. Nothing is moving forward, though."

"Wow, sorry to hear you are having so much trouble with the builder. It truly looks amazing to us, but we are no experts," Carla smiled at Charles and accepted his hand in helping her into the dinghy. "Enough sad tales," the Englishman tried to change the topic. "I hope you have heard about the Jump Up on the beach on Hog Island tonight. We are sponsoring the event. I will see you and your friends there."

Chapter 24

One Last Party

The CAR sailors were excited about one last party on the beach and determined to make the best of the fleet's imminent dispersal. "How many people are here, I didn't expect that," Hanna looked around to spot some friends in the almost complete darkness, only broken by a few open fires on the beach and a single lantern over the bar.

Peter pulled her toward the swings where the crowd of CAR children was playing, loosely supervised by their parents. "Hey, Hanna, Peter, good to see you, where are you off to next?" Kirsten from "Andante" wanted to know. The established CAR couples took a huge interest in the blossoming romance between Hanna and Peter. "Back across the pond eventually," Hanna said, "But first a season of charter tours here in the Caribbean, we won't leave for Europe before May." "We?" somebody cheekily asked. Peter grinned and answered: "I can conduct most of my current business remotely, via email and skype, so will stay on "Thea" as first mate for the time being." There was a spontaneous round of applause on that announcement. Carla gave her friend a quick hug. Steve and Peter joined the girls and the four of them moved to the beach, happily chatting. Everybody was here.

"Hi mister, don't be so pushy, there is enough for all," Carla smiled at Soren, the Chinese boat's co-skipper, who was trying to edge into the narrow gap next to her at the bar. "Great that you also made it here, are you still on "Hanseatic"? Soren smiled back: "Yes, my friend Sven and I had some differences, but eventually got over them. I feel sorry for him. He is here as well, over there at the beach. Very old friends don't give up on each other. But the best news is that Sven has sold the boat to a hotel family on the island. They will use it for taking guests out, we have delivered it to this bay for them. They wanted an outstanding looking boat, and "Elbe" certainly is that." "What a result for your friend, the local family wouldn't be the Dwyers by any chance?" Carla asked. "Yes, that's their name, how do you know?" Soren was surprised. "I have met Charles Dwyer and heard about their high-end concept, that boat fits the idea perfectly," Carla said. With four rum punches and a jug of lemonade on a tray, Carla rejoined her group.

"What have you guys decided about your information about Sven and "Saiche's" rudder stock? I have just spoken to Soren and he has forgiven his friend," Carla asked Peter after handing him a punch. Peter hesitated, looked at Hanna and answered: "We have given it a lot of thought and decided to stay mumm, not report it. It would damage the guy's reputation for good and finish off his business, I don't want that on my conscience. I might have a quiet chat to him and suggest he seek help." "He has sold his boat to the Dwyers, so should be a lot happier and hopefully will sell a few more of these beautiful boats," Carla told them, and Steve nodded and said: "This sounds like a good outcome for a bad situation."

"Let's have something to eat, I am starving, and the queue has shrunk," Peter suggested and they joined the crowd under the make-shift tent. The food was way better than the usual Jump Up standard, there was the obligatory chicken and rice but also delicious smaller nibbly things. Rum punch and beer were flowing freely thanks to the Dwyer family. Hanna was only two spots from being served, eying the lamb skewers, when somebody tapped her on the shoulder. "Elsbeth!" Hanna exclaimed, "And Pavel, what are you doing here, when did you get out, shouldn't you be resting?" Elsbeth hugged her friend tightly and started to cry. Pavel was leaning heavily on Elsbeth, his face gaunt and pale, but he tried a sheepish grin.

Before Hanna could ask any more questions he said: "I owe you an apology and thanks for what you did in St Vincent, we both are extremely relieved you helped Elsbeth out there. All this was a wake-up call for me, sorry I have been an asshole in the past."

Hanna couldn't believe her ears, could the man be totally changed by this nightmare? Hopefully it would last. Hanna smiled at him conciliatory while Peter pushed a chair under his bum so Pavel could rest. Peter then put a beer in the Pole's hand with the words: "I hope this does not interfere with your pain killers, my friend, cheers." Curious to see what the story was with Pavel, Carla and Steve approached the little group and they all settled at the water's edge on a collection of old chairs. Pavel wanted to get everything off his chest, it seemed, he couldn't stop talking. "I have made a few dumb mistakes and just want to clear things up now with you all, so I can move forward with a half-way clear conscience," he said.

Carla was stunned when she heard it had been Pavel who had pushed her off the cliff at the Toga party. "I was watching the courier in a working boat dropping off the packages on "Gdynia". I had anchored her in the bay for the night and did not want Carla to take photos or later question why I was anchored there, and not in the marina like the other CAR participants. I panicked a bit and just pushed you, Carla, I am really sorry, you could have really hurt yourself and I am glad you didn't." Steve glared at Pavel, but Carla took his hand and said: "As long as you promise never to deal with drugs again I might forgive you. But tell me, was that you by any chance who scared me in Bequia, rummaging around in the ferry?" "Yes, sorry again, I was paying the courier there after getting some money from the bank. I can't believe I got involved in something like that, so stupid. It was a narrow escape thanks to Elsbeth and Hanna." He looked at Elsbeth who stroked his arm.

But Pavel hadn't finished: "And one last thing. I hope you are happy to hear, Elsbeth and I are getting married. After what we have been through together, her falling overboard, the attack in St Vincent, the drugs, my hospital stay. It just feels right, we have found comfort in each other. To my surprise she said yes when I asked her." Elsbeth beamed and showed the diamond ring on her finger. "Wouldn't have been easy to find a ring like that anywhere here," Carla chided. Everybody cheered, clapped, there was hugs and congratulations. "I think we need more drinks to celebrate this happy ending, just help me here, Pete" Steve said and pushed through the crowd to the bar. Carla all of a sudden remembered her children, and guiltily walked to the swings where the CAR kids were playing some game. "We are over there at the beach, darling, if you need something, and watch out for your sister," she told Leif and moved back towards the hut.

Most of the CAR families and friends were at the beach by now and having a ball, together for the last time, talking, playing, eating and drinking. Soon it was close to midnight. "I am tired, darling, happy to take the kids back to the boat, it is way past their bed time anyway. You just stay on, I am sure somebody will drop you back to the boat." Steve often got tired of the chit chat at parties after a while and didn't mind getting the children into bed. Carla smiled at Steve, rounded the reluctant children up and gave everybody a good-night kiss before they climbed into the dinghy.

By now chairs had been cleared away on some even ground near the hut, and people had started dancing. Carla dragged Hanna and Peter onto the dance floor and they boogied away to hits from the 80s and 90s. Carla had the best of times, she loved dancing. An hour later she felt hot and sweaty and needed a drink.

"Carla, how are you? You seem to be enjoying yourself, I saw you dancing!" Charles Dwyer smiled his big, charming smile and added: "You look thirsty. We should be drinking champagne, I'll go up to the resort and get some!" "I must be bright red in the face," she said. "And you must be reading my mind, some cold champagne would be perfect now." Carla quite enjoyed the hotelier's attention, he had such an old-world charm about him that was rare nowadays. She looked around at the thinning crowd and watched Sabine Kellermann scoop her boys up from a beach lounger. "Very late for such small children," she thought. "Hopefully some crew guy will drive her to the boat so she won't have to ask her difficult husband." Speaking of the devil, Thomas Kellermann made another beeline for Carla with the usual aggressive expression on his face, slightly dulled down by too much alcohol. "Not another scene, mate, we just about had it with you," "Dania"'s bodyguard Nathan unsettled Kellermann by stepping very close to the German. Kellermann took one look at Nathan's serrated ear, bitten off in an army brawl, and turned away. Slowly he ambled toward the new resort, along the narrow path through the dense Caribbean bush.

Carla was wondering what had happened to Charles and the champagne, and also had to admit she was curious about the German. What was he doing at the resort? Following an alcohol-fuelled impulse, she set off for the resort after him, waving at Hanna on the dance floor as she left. She at least had the good sense to stay far behind Kellermann to remain undetected. Fortunately, Charles or his resort management had switched the lights on along the path and outside the resort.

Carla crept into the grand entrance hall of the main building, having lost sight of Kellermann moments before. The dark hall felt deserted and eerie, reminding Carla of the jungle ruins in the Jurassic park movies. Although this building was sparkling new. "Enter stage, a few raptors on the right," she joked to herself. "Where would the kitchen be, maybe in the back here, that's probably where Charles would get the champagne," she mused, walking along a dark corridor through huge doors into something that looked like a ballroom. She was glad that she was wearing sailing shoes that made no noise. Trying to adjust her eyes to the darkness in the room suddenly she was blinded by a light. Somebody was shining a torch directly into her eyes from close by.

"Now, now, who have we here, our curious little journalist again. You are such trouble, lady! I just about had it with your snooping." To Carla's horror Kellermann pulled out a small gun and started waving it at her. "This guy is completely insane," she thought, all of a sudden sober and quite scared, trying to inch back into the space behind the shining grand piano. "Now, Thomas, let's not overreact here, I've done nothing to harm you," Carla tried to sound confident. "I'm not so sure about that. What a shame you just can't stay away. I am afraid you will have a little accident very soon." With those slightly slurred words, and still aiming the gun at Carla, Kellermann grabbed a big jerry can of petrol. Where did that come from in the ballroom, Carla wondered, he must have hidden it near the building before.

"I am going to create a little insurance claim here. My client, the builder has just upped the building insurance on the place, as it is almost complete and worth a small fortune. Serves those pompous Dwyer guys right if everything goes up in flames, boom!" Carla gave a start, frantically looking for an exit without raising his suspicion. Kellermann moved toward the big doors, pouring the petrol behind him. He would lock the doors for sure, how could she get out? Where was Charles? Carla moved closer to the big windows.

With a mad laugh Kellermann flipped a match into the petrol and backed out through the big doors. The petrol erupted in a fiery explosion-like blast. The ballroom's interior, chairs, cushions, curtains quickly caught fire. The searing heat was almost unbearable within seconds. Carla didn't even try to reach the doors, Kellermann would certainly have barricaded them from the other side. "Stay calm!" she told herself and looked around for an exit. The windows looked solid but were only single glazing in this climate. Carla spotted a big flower vase and threw it at a window. The vase smashed into pieces but the window stayed intact. Carla frantically looked for something else. She spotted a candelabra, a modern one, not silver but still made from some sort of metal. Carla started hammering the window, lifting it like a clump over her head and smashing it into the glass. But nothing happened. Maybe it was bullet-proof, she thought. Smoke had by now filled the room, Carla was coughing, her eyes streaming.

All of a sudden she felt somebody grab her shoulder. "Carla, this way, through the kitchen!" Charles Dwyer took her hand and pulled her toward the other end of the room. They could hardly see through the flames and smoke. Charles pushed her through an invisible door in the far right corner of the ballroom. They ran past some serving areas and burst through a metal door into the open. Carla collapsed on some logs behind the building, coughing her heart out. "Thank god I found you, I heard you trying to smash the window. The fire brigade is on its way from Grenada, let's hope they will arrive on time," Charles said once they had recovered a bit. "Thanks for getting me out of there," Carla managed to say. Charles took his mobile phone out of his pocket and started making calls. Carla was surprised at what speed the local police arrived by boat, the station couldn't have been far. Charles soon told her that Kellermann in his drunken madness had not escaped but just driven back to his boat and gone to bed. To Sabine's surprise three police man woke them up at 5 am, handcuffed Thomas and led him to a police RIB.

The next morning dawned sunny and beautiful as Caribbean mornings do. Carla's family had let her sleep in after the night's dramas. Carla knew she looked bad when she saw Steve's shocked face, climbing down "Dania"s companionway around 4 am, all sooty and smelling of smoke. She had given a brief account of what had happened and fallen into her bunk. When she woke up at 10.30 her throat was sore and her arms were hurting. Both kids launched themselves at her and they had a huge family cuddle. Next she jumped over the side to clean the soot off.

At breakfast Steve smiled at her and said: "Charles has already been here, enquiring about you, but I didn't want to wake you. He looked a bit worse for wear like you. I sincerely thanked him for saving your life. He was very nice, just concerned you got entangled in his conflict with Kellermann. Looks like the main building with the ballroom burned down completely, he said it would take some time to rebuild that but the UK builder is keen and ready, and hopefully the insurance will cover some of the cost. It will delay the opening further but the main thing is that nobody got hurt."

Carla right at this moment was not interested in hearing more about the resort and its problems, she was just happy to be safe and with her family. "Let's go sailing, folks, a nice reach to Grenada Marine as we had planned. I think I've seen enough of Hog Island," Carla smiled at her children and gave Steve a kiss.

Made in the USA
Charleston, SC
02 September 2016